Praise for *Silver in the Wood*

"It is easy to praise flash and sparkle, but the beauty of the simple and lighter-than-air is more difficult to capture. *Silver in the Wood*'s sparkle is that of clear water, its flash the snap of a crackling fire . . . like returning to a dream long forgotten or a song half remembered."

—Alexandra Rowland

"Tesh's characters and mythology are exquisitely crafted. . . . This fresh, evocative short novel heralds a welcome new voice in fantasy."

—*Publishers Weekly*

"Somewhere between fairy tale and myth, only it's the kind of myth that is probably true."

—*Smart Bitches, Trashy Books*

"Find a quiet place in a nearby wood, listen to the trees whisper, and thank the old gods and new for this beautiful little book, of which I intend to get lost in again and again."

—*Book Riot*

"Tesh lured me into her rich fairy-tale narrative with the warmth and strangeness, then hooked me on her intricate characters."

—Kerstin Hall

"A splendid piece of work, self-contained enough to be a perfect use of the novella form, rich enough to tingle on the skin, direct and meaningful enough to be read aloud as a bedtime story."

—Locus

BOOKS BY EMILY TESH

DROWNED COUNTRY

COUNTRY

EMILY TESH

A TOM DOHERTY ASSOCIATES BOOK

NEW YORK

DROWNED COUNTRY

Copyright © 2020 by Emily Tesh

Cover image by David Curtis
Cover design by Christine Foltzer

Edited by Ruoxi Chen

A Tor.com Book
Published by Tom Doherty Associates
120 Broadway
New York, NY 10271

www.tor.com

Tor® is a registered trademark of
Macmillan Publishing Group, LLC.

ISBN 978-1-250-75659-6 (ebook)
ISBN 978-1-250-75660-2 (trade paperback)

First Edition: August 2020

for Luke
no crossbow this time

Drowned Country

I

The Demon of Rothling Abbey

THORNGROVES SHROUDED GREENHOLLOW HALL.
Blackthorn and hawthorn, holly and briar, carpets of
stinging nettles in case anyone missed the point. Adders
moved in that dark tangle. Crawling, stinging things skit-
tered along branches. Silver had a good line in alarming
spiders going.

Thin branches pressed up against the library windows,
tapping and tapping as if asking permission to come in.
No sunbeam had managed to penetrate in months.

On a Tuesday afternoon in April, a shudder of recog-
nition went through the whole mess. Silver was lying on
the dusty floor of the mediaeval great hall, staring at the
vaulted ceiling, contemplating making it sprout. Everything sprouted if he wanted it to. There was a healthy
crab apple demolishing its way through the ceiling and
floor of what had once been a whitewashed ground-floor
bedroom in the east wing. Crooked branches laden with
white blossom and sour fruit together thrust from bro-

ken windowpanes. The tree had been in both blossom and fruit for months and it was not happy. Silver was not happy either. Sometimes he went and sat in there and felt sorry for himself.

Other places Silver felt sorry for himself: his study, which as all the servants had left months ago was a mess; his library, which was hardly better; his bedroom, where mistletoe hung from the bedposts like midwinter baubles; and of course the floor of the great hall, where the cold of the ancient stones seeped into his back and the moss was spreading lusciously along the cracks between them. He sat up when he felt the shuddering demand go through the Wood. His outline remained on the stones where he had lain sketched in yellow-white lichen. There were several similar man-shapes scattered around the empty room.

"Behold my ghosts," said Silver out loud. He was in the habit of talking to himself now. He had tried maintaining a dignified silence for a while, and discovered that dignity counted for very little without an audience. These days he chattered, muttered, sang, read aloud when he bothered to read. He read much less than he used to.

The tangle of Greenhollow shuddered again. Silver imagined himself a spider in the web, feeling the threads tremble. "What," he said crossly, "what is it?"

Nothing.

"*What?*"

Something moved in the corner of his vision. He turned his head and glared at the shadows. The thorn-dryad Bramble gathered herself out of the nothingness and stepped into the room.

She hadn't been able to do that until the roof started crumbling. The fact that she could do it now was the one thing that might make Silver consider attempting to repair the roof.

"Get out," he said.

She fixed her sungold gaze on him. Silver refused to feel embarrassed about the fact that he was wearing the ragged remains of what had been one of his better shirts, and no socks or shoes. He had once prided himself on being well turned out. He wriggled his toes against the flagstones. A man shouldn't have to wear shoes in his own house if he didn't want to.

"But this is not a house," said the dryad, so he'd said that aloud.

"Get *out*."

Instead the dryad paced closer. She walked in long springing steps that cracked the stones beneath her feet. Little gasping patches of holly sprang up where her toes pressed down into the dust of the ancient flags, two or three leaves and a spray of berries each time. It looked as though the bodies lined in lichen had started bleeding.

Silver did not flinch away from her. She was a powerful and dangerous and strange creature, one of the mysteries of the Hallow Wood, unique even among her tree-sisters, but she did not frighten him. Nothing very much frightened him. Was he not the Lord of the Wood, nearer demigod than mortal man, master of time and seasons, beasts and birds, earth and sky?

"Your mother is here," said Bramble.

Silver froze.

After a long silence he managed, "Make her go away."

Bramble folded her arms. The human gesture did not suit her stiff shape, yet it struck Silver with a startling, painful familiarity. He knew just where she had learned that pose, and that frown, and that air of patient, half-amused disapproval. She showed no sign whatsoever of being in a rush to remove Adela Silver from the premises.

Silver scowled at her. He reached out to the wood himself, but the threads of its power slipped away from him. Rather than additional curtains of thorns springing up around the boundaries of Greenhollow Hall, the ones that were already there started to recede. The dryad was extraordinarily strong, and her relationship with the wood was peculiar; even a man with more than a couple of years' half-hearted experience making use of the power of the Hallow Wood might have struggled to match her. Silver gave up quickly. As the wall of thorn bushes gave way before the interloper, he felt a light tread in the soil, the swish of a severe skirt in the dew.

This was embarrassing. Silver was the lord of his own wood. He was the owner of his own *house*. And he was a grown man of twenty-five years. There was no reason his own mother should strike him with as much terror as if he were a naughty schoolboy caught scrumping.

"Oh, very well," he said, trying to pretend it had been his own idea all along. "Good of you to let me know, Bramble. Run along now."

The dryad stared at him a moment longer. She tipped her head very slightly to one side.

A wave of rot-scent rolled across the great hall as toadstools erupted through the flagstones and shelves of fungus spread themselves across the walls. The lichen-men vanished under the onslaught. Overhead the vaults of the ceiling erupted into greenery, and shafts of light pierced through as the roof finally, decisively, collapsed.

Silver put his hands over his head. It took a while for the rumbling echoes of falling masonry to die away.

Bramble smirked at him, showing pointed brown teeth, and disappeared.

Silver groaned.

"I paid a substantial sum of money for this place, I'll have you know!" he called out. He very much doubted the dryad even knew what *money* was, and it wasn't as if he could sell Greenhollow anyway. But *still*. He looked around in some despair. He was twenty-five years old, he still had some good clothes somewhere, probably, and he was the native demigod of an ancient forest kingdom; but just then he felt altogether defeated by rubble, by toadstools, and by the fact that Mrs Silver was certain to do no more than sniff faintly at the whole.

Moisture dripped from the walls and highlighted the subtle brown striations of the shelf fungus.

Silver contemplated reaching out to the Hallow Wood and attempting to turn his shattered home into a slightly more aesthetically pleasing ruin, or at any rate something he could pretend he had done on purpose, but he had never been able to lie to his mother anyway. Let her sniff. At least this way she could not invite herself to stay.

～

Silver met his mother on the steps of the Hall. He had run to his bedroom and thrown on a less horrific shirt, a countryman's tweed jacket which did not fit him because it was not his, and some socks and shoes.

"Mother!" he said in his most charming tone of voice as she approached. "What a delightful surprise! I . . ." He had to stop and swallow hard as he got a good look at her.

"I hope the journey was not too uncomfortable . . . ?" he managed.

Mrs Silver paused. She looked him up and down. "Henry," she said.

No one used Silver's given name. He tried to stand up straighter in the shapeless tweed jacket, and to give her the same treatment in return. She was wearing her second-best dark grey dress, which she often wore for travelling. She had retrimmed the wrists with a new lavender ribbon. Her black-caped lady's coat was adorned at her shoulder with a heavy silver brooch. Her hat was dove-grey with lavender trim. The effect was sombre in the extreme. Silver had never dared to ask her if she was *really* still mourning his father or if she just found the sober attire of the widow convenient for her purposes. Hunting monsters could be a messy business. Bloodstains hardly showed on black.

Her left hand rested on a cane. Silver had watched her walk up the well-paved drive with it, the strong stride he remembered replaced with a firm step, a halt, a decisive *tap*, and a second, more careful step. The cane itself was dark, elegant wood—not native, Silver noticed automatically, as he often did now—and tipped with silver. Silver wrenched his gaze away from it and back to Mrs Silver's eyes.

His mother's pale gaze had unnerved him all his life and this occasion was no exception. Almost at once he had to refocus on her forehead (newly careworn), her nose (unchanged; a familiar hatchet), her mouth (a straight unreadable line).

"Are you quite finished?" Mrs Silver said.

"Mother," Silver said faintly.

"Perhaps," she said, "you would like to offer a crippled old lady somewhere to sit."

Silver's mouth opened.

"*And* some breakfast," Mrs Silver added. "I have been travelling through the night."

Silver took a deep breath. "Of course. And—"

"I did not bring any travelling companions, before you ask. Mr Finch remains in Rothport."

"In Rothport?" said Silver. It was a seaside town a hundred and twenty miles to the northeast. His mind conjured, almost without his wishing it, a picture of Tobias Finch at the seaside; Tobias Finch emerging demurely from a bathing-machine, perhaps in striped flannel, or perhaps not—dear God. He wrenched his thoughts away from this entirely unprofitable train of thought. Tobias Finch was nothing to him.

"Henry," said Mrs Silver, thankfully distracting in her disapproval, "I am extremely tired. You will be good enough to see to my requests at once. Somewhere to sit down, and something to eat." She looked up at the battered frontage of Greenhollow, almost entirely hidden by a solid wall of creeping ivy. Her glance raked it up and down exactly the same way she had looked at Silver himself. Then she sniffed. "I assume that tea is beyond you."

~

Silver, defiantly, served his mother with small beer from the cellar and a plateful of sour apples, which he set very precisely down in the middle of the library table between them. Mrs Silver looked at the plate, looked at the shabby state of Silver's library, and drank a fastidious sip of the beer. She had not said a word as she picked her way across the fungus-crowded ruin of the great hall. "Well," was all she said now.

The silence lengthened. Silver knew this tactic intimately but crumpled anyway. "Well, what?" he said.

"Your father also liked to sulk," said Mrs Silver.

"I am not *sulking*," said Silver.

"I cannot think what else to call it," Mrs Silver said, "when a healthy young person insists on building himself a *thorn-girt fortress* and sitting in it consuming nothing but sour fruit and small beer for months on end. I blame myself. I should not have permitted you to read so many fairy tales as a boy."

"*Mother.*"

"If you are picturing yourself as a sort of Sleeping

Beauty, Henry, I regret to inform you that you have failed," Mrs Silver said. "You do not appear to be asleep, and you most certainly are not beautiful. Perhaps you would like me to cut your hair."

"No!" Silver said. He summoned up a glare. "I do not expect you to understand, madam, the effects of the Hallow Wood on a gentleman's constitution—"

"Mr Finch's constitution by that argument should have been considerably more affected than yours over the years," Mrs Silver said, "and yet I recall that he managed to keep himself—and his dwelling—presentable." She took another sip of the beer and added, without mercy, "And clean."

"*Mother.*"

"I have had various causes to be ashamed of you in the past, my son," she went on calmly, "but your *appearance* has never been one of them before."

"You can't *cut my hair*. I'm not a child."

"Oh, are you not?" Mrs Silver picked up a crab apple, took a bite, made a face at the taste, and took another. She chewed and swallowed. "My mistake."

"Why are you here?" Silver said. "What do you want?"

"Your assistance," she said.

"My what?"

"With a case." As if that hadn't been obvious. "A rather curious case, and one that is causing us a good deal of difficulty. You shall have to accompany me back to Roth-port."

"I can't go to Rothport," said Silver at once. "I can't leave the wood."

"Don't lie to me, Henry," said Mrs Silver. "I know perfectly well that you can go wherever you please, provided your *wood* has been there at some point in the last ten thousand years."

"I—"

Mrs Silver clicked her tongue.

Silver subsided. He probably could go to Rothport. They both knew it, just as they both knew perfectly well the real reason Silver was hesitating. "I can't imagine what use I could be to you," he said, a last attempt. He heard the tone of his own voice—reluctant, *not* sulky, thank you—and was irritated; he was playing into her hands. He made himself sit up straight and meet her familiar eyes. He even pasted on an easy smile. "Between your expertise and T—and Mr Finch—surely there is nothing missing from the practical folklorist's arsenal."

"You possess certain qualities that both of us lack," said Mrs Silver calmly. "This creature is cunning, ancient, and strong. I have no doubt that Mr Finch and I could deal with the problem ourselves, in time, but I fear we do not have time." She took another sip of the beer. She had said all this as neutrally as if she were commenting on the weather. She remained just as neutral as she added, "A young woman's life is at stake."

"Good *God*," said Silver, "how heartless you sound."

"Would histrionics on my part incline you to be less selfish?" Mrs Silver said. "If so, I am willing to oblige. The young lady's name is Maud Lindhurst. She is twenty-one years old. She disappeared a week ago, and Tobias and I have been there five days. He believes we are dealing with a vampire. A very *old,* very *clever* vampire. Even he has seen only a few of the type. They tend to avoid the domains of"—her voice went, if anything, even drier—"their natural rivals."

Neither of them said anything else for a moment. Silver glanced around as if the woodland's former master might step any moment from the shadows, grey-cloaked and glimmering and utterly cruel. Fabian Rafela had not, of course, been a vampire. He had been something much worse.

The table between them put out a few comforting green tendrils, wrapping them around Silver's fingers. Silver rubbed his index finger and thumb together across them. The library might be a wreck now but he had seen to the furnishings when he first purchased Greenhollow; the table was imported dark mahogany, rather beautiful. He could feel, distantly, the heat it wanted, the light. "You won't be happy rooted here," he murmured.

When he looked up, his mother's pale eyes were fixed on his face and her expression was strange.

Without letting himself think too much about it—Tobias, in Rothport, on the trail of something old and cunning and cruel and strong, strong enough that Silver's *mother* had actually *asked* for *help*—Silver sat back in his chair and spread his hands.

"Well, madam," he said, "you know how I hate to disappoint you."

~

Rothport curled up the grey coastal cliff like an inverted question mark.

Rothling Abbey, a gigantic ruin in the local black stone, dominated the headland. On clear days—which this was not—it was visible for miles out to sea. A road wound up towards it, lined with crooked houses on either side, but stopped at the modern church built a little further down the hill. The bulk of the town hugged the harbour, where two-masted doggers with folded sails huddled out beyond the long grey pier, along with a handful of bobbing modern tugs with dark smokestacks. A thin strip of foul-smelling sand was in evidence at the apex of the harbour's curve, and some brave soul had put up a large red parasol there to shade nonexistent visitors from the nonexistent sun. Stray spitting raindrops pattered on the red canopy and left spreading ripples on the dark surface of the sea. On that April afternoon, Silver stepped down from the hire carriage ahead of his mother, meaning to help her down, and then halted.

A memory that was only half his whispered to him that the ocean had not been there so long. There had been a broad valley, and half a hundred little rivers, and an unbroken forest cradling half the world stretching all across that silted land. And then, when the world changed and the water rose, there had been islands still strung out like a chain. Silver could almost see them, each crowned with its last handful of trees.

"—*Henry*," said Mrs Silver, and Silver startled and turned to the sound of her voice.

Tobias Finch was at her side, holding her hand as she stepped down from the carriage.

Still half-mazed by a dream of rising oceans, Silver could only stare.

How had he forgotten the *size* of the man?

Tobias dwarfed Silver's mother. He also stood head and shoulders above Silver, who was not short. But it was not just his height that struck one's attention; it was the broadness along with it, the deep chest, the powerful shoulders, the profound solidity of a man who even now seemed more a feature of the landscape than a human being. Tobias might have been carved out of the Rothport cliff. He might have stood like Rothling Abbey on the headland, blasted and unbowed for a thousand years. Silver felt small, shabby, flimsy, looking at him.

His hair was short now. Maybe Silver's mother had cut it. He wore sideburns and a neat moustache instead of the full beard he had sported when Silver first met him. He was less brown too than he had been a year ago; it had been a cold and sunless winter. In fact he looked every inch the well-set-up modern man. His shoes were shined; his hair was combed; his dark coat was good quality and fitted him well. Silver detected his mother's handiwork in that. He could not justly object. He entirely understood the urge to put Tobias's enormous and handsome form in decent clothes; hadn't he been generous himself, when he'd had the opportunity?

He stood up straighter, wishing now he'd had the sense to protect at least *some* of his own good clothes from his self-indulgent ruin of Greenhollow Hall. He thoroughly regretted wearing the too-large tweed jacket. But if nothing else, Silver prided himself on his ability to smile and speak well: so he smiled, as if they had never quarrelled and never parted and were in fact no more than casual acquaintances in the first place, and he said, "Mr Finch. A pleasure to see you again."

And already some imp in his thoughts was murmuring: *It has been nearly two years. Perhaps, now that he sees you—*

Silver pushed the thought down so it would not show on his face, and smiled at Tobias with, he hoped, the air of a man who had not been sulking for most of the time they had been apart. Nothing so unattractive as self-pity. But Tobias's hazel-green eyes flicked over Silver once, and he only nodded to him. "Morning, Mr Silver" was all he said.

A lock of his combed hair fell across his brow. Silver's hand twitched with the unacceptable desire to tuck it back into place, and he had to glance down. Tobias didn't seem to notice it, or the tweed jacket Silver was wearing, or anything at all; foolish of Silver, probably, to expect the man to even remember a garment he hadn't cared to take with him two years ago. He let go of Mrs Silver's hand to pick up her travelling case. He passed her cane to her as well. He had always been a man of few words. Who knew better than Silver how firm Tobias's reserve could be? Who knew better that under that implacable wall of reserve he had as much feeling as a hundred more demonstrative fellows? Perhaps, if Silver exerted a little patience, he might gain access to what lay beneath the surface. It had worked before, he told himself firmly. Hadn't it worked before?

The sea breeze picked up a little. Silver felt it tug at his dishevelled hair, his shapeless coat. The brim of Mrs Silver's hat bounced in the fresh air. The salt-and-fish smell of a minor harbour town rolled over the three of them. Tobias turned his back to Silver as he offered Mrs Silver his arm to help her walk up the hill.

For a snivelling and pathetic moment, Silver considered being jealous of his own mother.

Absurd. Embarrassing. He could do better.

It was not, he told himself, that he expected to win Tobias *back*. But there was nothing wrong with putting one's best foot forward.

"Well, madam, I am here and I am in your hands," he said, coming up on Mrs Silver's other side. He did not offer his arm; her stern grip on her cane told him it would not be welcome. "Let us by all means see to the happy resolution of the peculiar case of Maud Lindhurst."

~

The Lindhursts were a well-off older couple, living in one of the crooked houses on the hill. Their money would be in coal or cotton or wool or something; Silver had no interest in the matter. Thankfully, he barely had to speak to the pair of them. He got an impression of red-eyed helplessness from the mother, pompous terror from the father, and polite handshakes all round. Then Mrs Silver shut the three of them in the family dining room.

It was a substantial and gloomy apartment. Between the massive table, the carvers and dining chairs, the sideboards and ornamental cabinets and overblown mantelpiece, there was scarcely room for one person to sidle in, let alone three. As if all that were not bad enough, there was also an upright pianoforte crammed into the corner. The only way a person could possibly play it would be if they were rail-thin enough to fit themselves into the miniscule gap where the stool was jammed next to the fireplace screen.

Tobias was too big for the room. It took him some effort to squeeze himself around the far side of the table, and he knocked over a candlestick with his elbow and looked worried by it. Mrs Silver took the carver at the table's head and sat with a little sigh of relief, setting her cane against the arm of the chair. Silver went to the window and threw open the dark green damask curtains, letting in some light if no air. This side of the house had a view of the church, squat and rather ugly, and the dark bones of the ruined abbey rising behind it like the carcass of a whale. Silver looked at it for a studied moment.

"A romantic spot," he remarked lightly. "The sort of place where one imagines Gothic maidens being menaced by dreadful demons. So." He turned, with his most charming smile, intentionally not aimed in any particular direction. "Tell me about this vampire."

The big dining table was covered in papers; Mrs Silver's looping handwriting predominated, but Silver could see a faded notebook full of a half-familiar scrawl, held open with a paperweight. The situation was serious if Mrs Silver had resorted to his father's records. There were also three or four books that he recognised; his own copies were in the dusty library at Greenhollow Hall. *De Stricibus et Lamiis;* that was an old chestnut. *Vampires, Ghouls, and Other Revenants: Some Continental Legends.* Silver picked that one up, meaning to flip through it—only wanting something to do with his hands—and found it had been covering up a pile of pencil sketches. The topmost one showed the face of an older man: bald, unsmiling, strikingly hawk-nosed, with piercing black eyes. Silver raised his eyebrows and picked it up. "Is this the creature? Your sketches have improved, madam."

"Mr Finch's work," said Mrs Silver.

Silver glanced at Tobias, surprised. He had never shown any signs of being artistically inclined in Silver's company. He found his eyes straying to Tobias's big hands, trying to imagine them holding anything as delicate as a pencil. "You have a gift, Mr Finch," he said.

Tobias said nothing. Silver watched him a moment longer, hoping. No.

Be patient, he reminded himself.

"The picture is a copy," said Mrs Silver, "of a portrait which hangs in the town hall. It supposedly shows a Mr Jameson Nigel, a gentleman of Rothport some fifty years ago. And *this*"—she moved the topmost sketch aside to reveal another, undoubtedly the same individual or a very close relative, though now he sported a powdered wig above the piercing black eyes and wore an embroidered doublet with a lace collar—"is a copy of an oil painting belonging to a local landowner, which he claims shows either a distant uncle or an old family friend of a distant uncle—he is not sure. Nor did he know a date, but by the clothing I imagine it must be two or three hundred years old. He gave the name as Sir Nigel Julian. And then *this*"—a third sketch, and here were the black eyes and hawk nose under a monk's tonsure—"comes from the church on the hill; a fresco, supposedly showing one of the early Abbots of Rothling—Abbot Julius the Black."

"An unsaintly looking fellow," Silver managed after a moment. If this was really their vampire, that made him nine hundred years old at least. Older than Tobias, who had been the Hallow Wood's servant for centuries before Silver took up its lordship. Older than anything Silver had ever met: unless you counted the Lord of Summer.

"Its looks are not my interest except insofar as they may help to identify the creature. Which brings us to tonight's attempt," said Mrs Silver. "We must locate the lair. If Maud Lindhurst is still alive, she is there. You, Henry—"

She explained. Silver reared back, affronted.

"You brought me here to be *bait*?" he said.

"Why else did you think I needed you?" said Mrs Silver. "The creature's habits are well known in Rothport. I even interviewed some older fishermen who recalled meeting it in their youth. It has a history of accosting handsome young men."

"But Maud Lindhurst—"

"—is a break in the pattern," said Mrs Silver. She did not say anything else. Silver, who had been familiar with his mother's profession since childhood, knew as well as she did that changes in a supernatural being's habits seldom portended anything good. In the corner of his eye he saw that Tobias had his hands knotted together on the table and his head bowed over them. He knew it too.

Still. "I rather thought," Silver said stiffly, "that you might need my help in some more *worthwhile* capacity, given my particular talents—"

"You are a capable researcher, but so am I," Mrs Silver dismissed him. "And any business too physically demanding for my present condition can be managed by Mr Finch much more effectively than *you*."

Silver had always striven to give his mother the impression that he was rather feeble, barely able in fact to lift anything heavier than a dictionary or perhaps his guitar, since he knew very well that otherwise he was likely to get dragged willy-nilly into activities involving a tiresome amount of running, fighting, and shooting. It was oddly irritating to find that he'd succeeded so well.

Not that Tobias *wasn't* more capable than he was. But Silver was not quite a nonentity, whatever his mother thought.

"So," he said, "I take it I am to stand around attractively all night, like a choice cut on display at the butcher's—I hope you can provide me with a better coat for it? Or am I to wear only my nightshirt? And then hopefully our friendly nine-hundred-year-old man-eater will drag me to his lair, at which point the pair of you will track me down and rescue either myself and Maud Lindhurst, or myself and what is *left* of Maud Lindhurst, or quite possibly what is left of both of us—"

"You can defend yourself," said Tobias softly.

Silver looked at him. Tobias's head had come up and his eyes were fixed on Silver's, for the first time in nearly two years. Silver had to suppress a shiver, an unaccountable sense that under the neat moustache and sideburns Tobias was still the same awesome and strange being whom Silver had first met. Nonsense. It was nonsense. *Silver* was awesome and strange; Tobias was a common mortal man. He was Mrs Silver's *employee*. His serious look should not have such a cataclysmic effect on Silver's composure.

"Will you provide me with a flint knife?" he managed, with rather weak sarcasm, hopefully fast enough that Tobias had not noticed his effect. Silver had no hope that he could keep it secret from his mother.

Tobias shook his head. "There's more life in you than a vampire can bear," was all he said. "The ones I met before, they couldn't hurt me."

"The few you met in your tenure as the Wild Man of Greenhollow were, I believe, considerably younger than this ancient," Silver said. "Younger and weaker."

"I'll be there," Tobias said seriously. He held Silver's gaze. "He won't have you long."

Silver's breath caught. After a moment he remembered to nod.

~

The sun was setting behind the hills. Eastward it was already dark; the low roar of the sea sounded out of black nothingness. Occasionally the sky spat out a few drops of rain and then changed its mind again. Silver had tried trading the shapeless tweed jacket that he had started wearing after Tobias left for a good broadcloth coat smelling faintly of mothballs which the Lindhurst parents had found on Mrs Silver's command, but it fit so poorly that as vampire-bait it hardly made a difference.

And the jacket was warmer.

Mrs Silver was not with them. She had been to Hallerton and back in less than two days, and her leg ached; she had retired to bed early. Silver had not realised until then how very much easier it was to have her there. But he gathered his courage. To walk through Rothport with Tobias Finch alone was perhaps an opportunity.

While he was struggling to think of an opening that was suitably airy without being flippant, Tobias said, "Have you eaten?"

"I have not," said Silver.

Tobias nodded and kept walking. His natural long stride was just slightly too fast to keep up with easily, but he adjusted quickly for Silver's pace when he noticed. He must be used to it by now, Silver supposed, if he was always giving Mrs Silver his arm as she hobbled about. He set that thought aside quickly. He did not like how real his mother's injury had suddenly become. He did not want to dwell on it.

Tobias led them down towards the pier. In a narrow and smoky shop on the waterfront he bought them each a slice of greasy fried fish wrapped in old news sheets. Silver watched him hand a couple of coins to the heavyset fellow behind the counter, determinedly not thinking of anything. They wandered down the pier—or Silver did, and Tobias followed him—to eat the fish. The heat of the double handful of newspaper kept Silver's hands warm; he burned his tongue on the first hot mouthful. He had not tasted anything like it in years.

It was impossible to pretend Tobias was not there. He did not push himself on Silver's attention, but he was simply too big to ignore. Silver half a dozen times nearly started to speak, but no line of conversation he could think of seemed right. In the end he made himself look out across the water awhile, as if he were meditating on the ocean's glories. A part of him watched himself do it and wanted to laugh: *Look at you, pretending to be so distant and unconcerned; the delightful young gentleman distracted by the splendours of Nature!*

In a competition of contemplative silences, against Tobias, Silver would always lose. "There was a forest here," he said when his tongue simply could not keep still another moment. What an inane thing to say. Greasy scraps of newspaper still clung to his hands though the fish was gone; he peeled them away and threw them in the water.

"The Wood?" Tobias said.

"Yes. I suppose so." Now Silver had brought it up, he could glimpse those islands again, hovering just beyond the edges of time; the darkness below the two of them might have been the broad waters, or it might have been the crowns of an endless expanse of trees.

"What happened to it?" Tobias said.

"It drowned," Silver said. The last of the sunset was fading from the world behind him; the night was very dark. "It drowned."

If Tobias answered, Silver did not hear it. A moment later he shook his head hard. The Hallow Wood asked nothing and offered nothing; it only was. Silver could contemplate the drowned forest at his leisure. Possibly he could even go for a walk in it. There were no precise rules to the way time behaved beneath the trees: *softening*, Tobias had called it, back when Silver had felt able to ask him questions of this sort.

But just now time did have demands to make of Silver. The likely fate of Maud Lindhurst grew darker every night she was missing. For her sake—or rather for the sake of Mrs Silver travelling overnight to ask, for Tobias with his head bowed over his knotted hands in the Lindhurst dining room—Silver would remain in this present moment, on the Rothport pier, with Tobias's big quiet form at his shoulder, and his hands covered in the faint greasy residue of fried fish.

He reached into his pocket for a handkerchief. When he'd wiped his hands, he almost turned to offer it to Tobias, only to find that the man had his own.

Of course he did.

"A moonless night," Silver said instead, to cover the moment. "Ideal for a vampire on the prowl. Mr Finch, I fear you shall have to follow me at a distance. I doubt our hungry friend will take the bait if you are hovering over it."

"All right," Tobias said.

"Loath as I am to lose the pleasure of your company," Silver said, "Miss Lindhurst must be our first concern."

"All right."

The conversation was as painful as picking one's way through a patch of nettles. But Silver with increasing despair could not see a way to start a better one. He had to make the attempt. "I hope," he said, "that any quarrels we may have had in the past can be put aside while we pursue this urgent matter."

Tobias looked at him for a moment, and there was, after all, a crack in his reserve. Someone who did not know him might not have seen it. Silver did know him, and so he knew that look. Tobias knew perfectly well that Silver was trying to wheedle his way around him, and he did not approve. His arms were folded in the gesture Bramble still copied from him, and his expression was shuttered, and Silver understood him perfectly: *Enough of that.*

37

So, that was that. He might as well have stayed at home in his thorn-girt fortress, pitying himself. Silver glanced away, pretending to consider the shadow-town he was about to wander through. Lights at windows and from the gaslamps on the high street up to the hill picked out the outlines of it even on this dark and damp evening.

"Keep to the shadows," said Tobias. Silver understood it for pity—no, for kindness, damn him, a kind and firm end to any foolish fantasy of repairing things. "He'll be in one of 'em."

"I know what I'm doing," Silver said.

He set off into the dark alone. He did not hear Tobias follow after him. He had always been surprisingly soft-footed for such a big man.

～

Rothport after dark was cold and damp, and it still smelled strongly of fish. It was also not a big place. If it had not been a stopping point on the coast between the coal mines of the north and the greedy maw of the capital, it would be little more than a fishing village. Rothling Abbey was of some minor historical interest, but not nearly enough to justify the difficulty of reaching the place. Not even the most enterprising of railwaymen had troubled himself to extend the lines out this far.

Silver walked up and down its handful of streets and alleyways, forcing himself to think of nothing, to set the sting of rejection aside. Two years he'd had to recover from this; why had he started hoping? It was only the surprise of seeing Tobias Finch again. Silver would not be undone by him, not now.

He smiled mildly at the occasional figures who loomed out of the dark at him, but all of them were ordinary locals. When the public houses closed, the exodus of the drinkers resulted in several such meetings. One gentleman did show signs of wishing to lure Silver into a darker corner, but Silver quickly identified him as a mortal bent on personal amusement, rather than a nine-hundred-year-old hellbeast desirous of Silver's lifeblood. At any rate, he turned positively green when Tobias materialised out of the shadows behind him. Silver rolled his eyes at the fellow's stammered apologies to both of them and did not bother to correct his misapprehension. He nodded to Tobias, one professional to another, and set off into the dark again with a sigh.

It was all very dull. This was what Silver had always loathed about his mother's approach to their one shared interest: how was it possible for the pursuit and discovery of marvels out of myth to be so thoroughly boring? Mrs Silver stripped romance and delight from everything; she looked upon the rarest and most extraordinary of beings rather as a rat-catcher looked upon rats. Perhaps she had been right all along. Perhaps Silver should have resigned himself already—resigned himself long ago—to a world that was essentially dry and unpleasant, where at the heart of every marvel there was just a skittering pest in the dark.

A little past midnight, Silver stood in the pool of light under one of Rothport's few streetlamps, wondering if he should have just gone out in his nightshirt after all. Or perhaps the vampire's historic tastes had changed so thoroughly that Silver was not suitable bait for it now; or perhaps it was entirely occupied with tormenting Maud Lindhurst and would not be abroad tonight.

Or perhaps after months of lurking in his thorn-girt fortress, Silver had lost his good looks on top of everything else.

He caught the peevish tone of his own thoughts and frowned at himself. He was not his mother; he would not be heartless. So Tobias Finch did not desire to repair their good relations; what had changed? Silver had not come here for him. He winced, catching his own thoughts in the obvious lie; why else had he come?

He had come, he reminded himself, because a young woman's life was at stake. Maud Lindhurst, twenty-one years old: he tried to picture her and came up with a mental portrait of a sweet blue-eyed creature in a white dress. Possibly she wore flowers in her hair. She was of an age to be Silver's younger sister. There, how could one fail to worry about Maud Lindhurst?

Something took hold of Silver's sleeve. He made a sound closer to a yelp than a manly cry of surprise.

A wild-eyed old man who smelled strongly of fish—did *anything* in Rothport not smell of fish?—was gazing up at him in some distress. He opened his mouth and said—

Unfortunately, the old tramp's local accent was so thick that it took several tries before Silver understood he was being given a terrible warning, and by that point he was trying not to laugh. "Thank you," he managed.

The tramp gesticulated fiercely and then pointed—to heaven? No, to the hill. "Beware!" he hissed, and then a garble of sounds that Silver after a moment interpreted as "The old Abbot likes fresh meat like you!"

"Thank you," he said. Of course, the ruined abbey. For no reason except sheer physical laziness Silver had been avoiding the steep road, half of it a stairway, leading up the hill. But he must have wandered through every other byway Rothport could offer by now; and where else to find a vampire but in a Gothic ruin?

"Beware!" cried the tramp again.

"Don't worry about it, there's a good fellow," said Silver, and reached for his purse only to remember that he didn't carry one any more. "I shall be most careful, I assure you."

He disentangled his sleeve from the ancient's trembling grasp, smiled at him, smiled too over his head at the tall form of Tobias, who hovered only a few yards off, plainly on the point of intervening. When Tobias did not smile back Silver looked away. In the puddle of light where he had been standing, he saw, tough dandelions had split the cobblestones and were poking their heads up towards the scatterings of April rain which hissed through the pool of lamplight. There would be yellow flowers in the morning.

Tobias was looking at the dandelions too. No, he wasn't. He was looking at the beggar, thoughtfully, and after a moment he went over to the man and took him gently by the arm and handed him a coin from his purse.

"All right," Silver said briskly, mostly to himself, and set off for Rothling Abbey.

~

In daylight, and on a warm summer's day, the ruins of Rothling Abbey might have been a pleasure to visit: one could bring a picnic, exclaim over the view, and possibly attempt some watercolours. On a clear and moonlit autumn night, assuming one had wrapped up warmly first, the spot might still have offered some delight to those who enjoyed shivering at a ghostly ambiance.

On that damp and overcast April evening, after puffing up the last of the hill in increasing misery, Silver heartily wished he'd never heard of the place. He would have liked nothing more than to be in a bed. A *soft* and *warm* bed, with clean sheets and a minimum of woodland adornment: so not his bedroom at Greenhollow Hall, where half the furniture was doing its best to take root. In fact Silver could not think where his ideal bed might be; only that wherever it was, he very much wanted to be in it, either asleep or in the company of—some person who was not Tobias Finch; some other person, a charming and well-read individual who found Henry Silver both interesting and impressive.

Tobias had reached the top ahead of him. He had passed Silver on the way up, his long strides eating up the steep hill as comfortably as if he were wandering through a meadow. He was not even breathing hard, but he had taken his coat off and laid it over the top of a nearby crumbled half-wall. When Silver forced his gaze up to meet his eyes—*must* the man be so *large*—Tobias gave him a silent, professional nod. Loops stitched on his belt held three sharpened wooden stakes.

Silver shuddered. Here was the other reason he disliked this sort of thing. He almost pitied the vampire.

Maud Lindhurst, he reminded himself, and he held the picture of the flowers she might wear in her hair so firmly in his thoughts that sprays of blossom began to uncurl themselves on the creepers which were anchored to the crumbling abbey walls, ghostly pale pink in the wavering moonlight.

The ruin was bigger than it had looked from the bottom of the hill. Silver took a deep breath, straightened his back, lifted his chin—the better to attract a bloodsucker—and set off towards the tumbledown cloisters. He felt a faint prickling discomfort as he advanced: for the first time in two years, his sense of the life and power of the Hallow Wood receded from him. It had been a very long time since trees had grown on this wind-blasted headland.

Something moved serpent-quick in the shadows.

"Silver!" Tobias roared behind him.

Silver startled, glanced both ways, and then flinched away from a sudden cloud of dust which a cold wind seemed to blow directly into his face. Even as he breathed it in he thought, *I should have held my breath*; then darkness rose around him, and he knew nothing for a time.

~

Silver woke up lying on some very cold stones. For a baffled moment he thought time had run away with him altogether and he was once again sprawling on the floor of his own great hall at Greenhollow.

Then he smelled the musty air and felt the prickling discomfort which told him his wood was much further away than he was used to. He said, out loud, "*Damn.*"

Nothing answered him. Tobias? What had become of Tobias? It was pitch-dark in here. Was this the vampire's lair? "Mr Finch!" Silver called out, and then, remembering, "Miss Lindhurst!"

Nothing. Silver struggled to his feet, reached out blindly with both hands, and discovered the room was a tiny dark cell. His hands touched an iron ring overhead—a trapdoor?—and his breathing quickened. Underground. He was underground. He gave the iron ring a hard tug and then attempted a shove. Neither had any effect.

Although he did not like to dwell on the matter, Silver was not fond of the dark, nor yet of confinement. He had been buried alive once. It did not live in his waking memory, but in dreams sometimes he still felt the cracking and churning of the earth, the twitching helplessness of the withered husk that Rafela had made of him, the force of strong roots pushing him down.

Damn, damn, *damn.*

Silver gritted his teeth and reached for the nearest things he could find. There was wild grass and heather, a scattering of gorse, and a tiny handful of determined survivors from what had once been a monks' garden. None of these things were the *Wood*; they did not know him, they did not answer to his demands.

"Oh God," Silver said. He could crack stone; he could overturn earth. He knew he could. Bramble had demolished half his *house,* by God. There was no need to panic. "Mr Finch!" he called out again anyway. But Tobias had *seen* it, he had shouted a warning, he had not been fast enough to save Silver from this imprisonment. Maybe it had killed him. Silver's mouth was dry; his hands shook. It was easy to forget how dangerous the monsters of legend could be. His indomitable mother walked with a limp now.

If it had killed Tobias, would Silver's mother come for him? She would. Silver, with shameful relief, knew that she always would.

And if it had killed Tobias, what would it make of Adela Silver?

"Shall I come back?" inquired a voice above him, interrupting these bleak thoughts.

The trapdoor was open. A slim figure was crouched over it, with the planks braced on her shoulder.

"Unless you'd rather stay down there," she said. "I suppose I should apologise." She didn't. "Come on, then, unless you'd rather sit around groaning."

~

The hand that helped Silver scramble out of the tiny cell was strong for all its softness. The room he emerged into was another cellar, no less dark in principle, but a merry glow came from a portable paraffin stove and tall golden stands held arrays of candles in the four stone corners. Silver blinked at the candlesticks. They had a distinct ecclesiastical air. He turned to the stranger.

"Miss Lindhurst?" he said.

"Maud," said the girl briskly. "Who the hell are you?"

Silver blinked. The only woman he had ever known to curse was his mother, and even that was very rare.

He was also staggered by the young lady's appearance.

She was as distant from the lovely and doleful waif of Silver's imagination as a hawk from a dove. Her hair was yellow—so far she matched the imaginary—but rather than a tastefully pastel blonde, it was a bold brassy guinea-gold colour, so bright one half suspected dye. Since Maud Lindhurst's appearance in every other respect said that here was a woman who did not care for outward show—the bright hair was wound up at the back of her head in a coil so firm and severe it was worthy of Silver's mother—Silver imagined it was natural. Otherwise, she was tall for a woman, with features too strong to be called pretty and too dull to be called striking: watery blue eyes, a long nose, a pinched little mouth. She was sloppily dressed in men's clothing, tough corduroy trousers and a white shirt with the sleeves rolled to her elbows. Silver was largely immune to the charms of young ladies in any case, but he did not think he had ever seen one less interested in being charming.

"Well?" she said.

"Miss Lindhurst, I really must protest—"

"I asked for your name, not your protestations," said Maud.

"Henry Silver," he said. "Miss Lindhurst, your parents—"

"Silver," said Maud. "Any relation to Alfred Silver?"

"My late father. I—"

"I liked his paper on the classifications of the supernatural. No one's bettered it since." She narrowed her eyes. "Didn't you have an article in the last *Folklore*? No, the one before. On the Hallow Wood. Rather coy, I thought."

"I *beg* your pardon."

"You plainly knew more than you were saying," said Maud, eyeing him with distaste. "Why pretend to be a scholar if you're going to keep secrets? You didn't mention the Wild Man once—anyone who knew anything about the Greenhollow matter would, unless there was something bloody odd going on." As she was eyeing him, she went on in much the same tone, "What on earth are you wearing?"

"*Miss Lindhurst,*" said Silver, exasperated, "your parents—at some considerable expense—have employed a pair of master monster-hunters to track you down after believing you to be *abducted* by a *vampire*—"

She snorted with laughter.

"—and I am here because I have no ability to say no to my mother, and my coat is none of your business, and—*what* have you done with Tobias Finch?"

She raised her eyebrows. "That depends. Is Tobias Finch the Wild Man of Greenhollow?"

While Silver floundered over how to answer *that* question, she went on, "Because I have the Wild Man, or someone who looks extremely like him, sleeping off a double dose in the undercellar next to yours."

"Miss Lindhurst," Silver said in his firmest manner. "I do not know what has possessed you to run away from home and take up residence in—I suppose this crypt is a remnant of the old abbey?—and assault strange gentlemen, but—" Good God, maybe she *was* possessed, or hypnotised, or whatever it was that vampires were supposed to do to their victims. Silver found it hard to imagine a young lady behaving this way of her own free will. Although he also found it hard to imagine the vampire whose dark passions were inclined towards young women who dressed up in unflattering costumes and criticised Silver's articles in *Folklore.*

"But?" said Maud, and then while Silver floundered her small mouth quirked up very slightly at the corner. If there was anything that was more charmless than a plain young lady who was shockingly direct with you, it was a plain young lady who was laughing at you. "Your Mr Finch is perfectly well. I probably *should* apologise." She still didn't. "I panicked. He'll wake up when it wears off."

"When *what* wears off?" Silver said. "What the hell did you do to us?" And *that* marked the first time he'd ever sworn in the presence of a lady, including his mother. Maud Lindhurst deserved it.

"Let me introduce you," said Maud, "to the Demon of Rothling Abbey. It's through here."

~

In a square stone sarcophagus on a platform surrounded by golden candlesticks lay a shrunken white corpse swaddled in a black shroud. There was a wooden stake thrust squarely through its chest. It had also been beheaded, but the head had then been gently placed next to its neck. It tilted unfortunately to one side, but there, rheumed with death, were the dark and staring eyes, and there the hawk nose, of Rothport's nine-hundred-year-old vampire.

"There he is," said Maud. "Old Julius. He preferred Julius to Nigel, really, though he answered to both."

"You knew him?"

"I used to play around the abbey ruins as a child," Maud said. "He would come out to watch me, when the evenings were long enough. I spoke to him a few times. I think he was rather sad, really." She said this without much feeling, as if she were discussing a distant great-uncle whom she had occasionally been forced to converse with at family gatherings. "I saw him with one of his handsome young men down in town once. They pulled the man out of the harbour the morning after. People said he fell in the water drunk and drowned."

"What happened to his hand?" The corpse's left wrist ended in a stump.

"Oh, I cut it off and powdered it," Maud said. "Vampire dust is a natural soporific. I thought it might be useful. And so it was, of course."

Silver took a deep breath and immediately wished he hadn't. He'd *breathed* the stuff. His stomach squirmed.

"You're not squeamish, are you?" said Maud, instantly dashing Silver's hope that she wouldn't notice. "I can't stand squeamishness. But I've got smelling salts in my things somewhere if you need them."

"No need," Silver managed. He was rather embarrassed. His mother and Tobias would both have looked calmly down at the monster's corpse without turning a hair, but Silver was not that sort. That had been a human being, once—long ago, perhaps, but—nine hundred years in the dark, creeping out at eventide to watch a child play—

Maud gave him a sceptical look but said, "Didn't you say you hunted monsters? He ate people, if that makes you feel any better. Quite a lot of them over the years, I imagine."

"My *mother* hunts monsters," Silver said. "I study the marvellous. It's not at all the same thing."

He turned away from the sarcophagus, scraping the remnants of his dignity together. "Very well, you are not the victim of a vampire. I grant, Miss Lindhurst, that you seem quite capable of looking after yourself. *Were* you abducted?"

"I climbed out of the window," Maud said.

"I see."

"I really should apologise," she said, and still didn't. "I see now that it would have been better to hide down here and wait for the pair of you to leave. I doubt you would have discovered the crypt after dark—the entrance is very well disguised—and by the time you came back in the morning, I would already have been gone. Only, I was above ground, taking measurements, and then . . . it was seeing *him* again that startled me."

Silver said nothing. He was good at drawing people into informative conversation; Maud, now she was attempting it, was plainly a rank amateur. She wanted to know about Tobias. Or rather, she *did* know about Tobias, know *something*; something about Greenhollow, something about the Wild Man, something about the Hallow Wood. And she wanted to know more.

Silver did not care for it at all.

"I would like to see Mr Finch now," he said.

"If you like," said Maud, and she couldn't even hide her disappointment properly.

~

Maud had indeed dragged Tobias into yet another sub-cellar of the sprawling hidden crypt. "There, you see?" she said, as the two of them looked down through the trapdoor. "He's perfectly well. Just asleep."

"Miss Lindhurst, you gave my companion a double dose of an untested soporific—"

"Of course it's not untested," she said sharply. "I tested it on myself. It's entirely safe. How else do you think I knew a dosage?"

"I *beg* your pardon?"

"I gave you enough to knock me out for an hour," she said, "since you're about my size: and I gave him twice as much, since he's about twice my size."

Silver stared at her, caught between admiring and appalled. "Young lady—"

She snorted. "Are you my *father*?"

"Miss Lindhurst—"

"Maud," said Maud, firmly. "I told you. Well, there he is. I half doubted it would work. Is he even human?"

"Entirely," said Silver, "I assure you." This was a strange view, here in this dank crypt surrounded by golden candlesticks and looking down as it seemed into the bowels of the earth where Tobias lay motionless. He had seen Tobias asleep before, of course. He had crept in the early morning from under that massive arm, unable to stop smiling even as spring called him up and away to walk the Wood. Oddly, he felt a fresh stab at the memory: not the self-pity he was so used to, but grief, real grief, for something lost.

The light from the candle Maud held at an angle illuminated the top of Tobias's head, the outline of his big shoulders in shirtsleeves. He was facedown and still, but he did not look smaller or more vulnerable; he looked fearsomely strong. Silver swallowed. Underground again. "Forgive me," he said, "but I find I *do* feel rather lightheaded. I must confess I dislike confined spaces. You heard my outburst earlier."

"Quite natural," said Maud, but her tone and expression spoke of amusement, and not a little pity. This girl had killed an ancient vampire to steal its crypt and then tested the effects of its powdered corpse on herself. She must have a stomach of steel. A little like Silver's mother, in fact—except that Silver's mother never allowed courage to get in the way of good sense.

Silver was counting on the fact that Maud, for all her obvious courage and intelligence, plainly had the common sense of a flea. Even *Tobias* had not wanted to hunt this vampire alone. The fact that she had succeeded was beside the point: what a lunatic risk to take! "I am sure you are right and he is perfectly well, but would you mind—forgive my nervousness—would you mind just checking his pulse for me? He is a very dear friend." Silver put all the sincerity at his disposal into his voice. It helped that it was close to the truth. *Friend* hardly described their connection, now, but if Silver forced a smile—

"If you insist," said Maud, and passed him the candlestick.

She swung herself down through the trapdoor as handily as any young sailor, plainly very comfortable in her corduroys and shirtsleeves. She crouched and pressed two fingers to Tobias's pulse for a moment. The candlelight picked out the bright gold of her hair in the gloom. "He's quite well, as I said," she said.

"*Mr Finch,*" said Silver.

He needn't have spoken. Tobias was already moving, erupting with surprising speed from the huddled pile where he had most certainly not been asleep—didn't Silver know what he looked like asleep?—facedown, the better to hide the flicker of his eyes. He grabbed Maud by the wrists—she barely had time to shout in surprise—and turned them around, pinning her to the ground with one strong hand, and his *other* hand went for his belt—

"Tobias, for the love of God!" Silver called out, and Tobias stopped with one of those sharpened stakes held at a professional angle over Maud's ribcage and looked up.

Silver said, "She's not our vampire."

"Was always a chance the beast would turn her," said Tobias, but he narrowed his eyes, dropped the stake, and put his hand to Maud's throat: that same careful check for a pulse, with a rather different intent this time. Then he nodded and let the girl go.

"Sorry, miss," he said. "Better to be safe."

Maud looked ever so slightly shaken as she scrambled to her feet. "Not as strong a dose as I thought, then."

~

And then they all sat down together in the ancient vampiric crypt, at what by now had to be two in the morning, and drank hot sugary tea out of cheap tin mugs.

Silver had to work to keep from cracking into dreadful laughter at the absurdity of it all. Maud had pointedly picked up a revolver while she was making the tea over the paraffin stove; it was in a pocket of those corduroys now. It was perfectly clear that she did not intend to be returned home by main force. Silver had no idea if the girl was capable of shooting a man and did not relish the prospect of finding out. She was certainly capable of beheading a vampire. He'd spotted the cleaver among her things.

So the three of them were sitting and chatting—well, Silver and Maud were sitting and chatting, and Tobias was sitting and not chatting—as if there were not a nine-hundred-year-old corpse in the next arched chamber. Maud's eyes kept flicking thoughtfully towards Tobias. He looked grim and troubled still. The prospect of killing a young girl turned vampire had distressed him; had been distressing him from the start, probably. Silver could see that now. He should have thought of it sooner. There had been a time when Tobias's silence and calm had not deceived him; when he had been able to tell what the big man was thinking. No longer, it seemed.

Maud, it turned out, could be coaxed into explanations. This was not a surprise. It was Silver's experience that most people could be persuaded to talk about themselves with very little effort. Tobias, with his natural reserve, had been a piquant exception from the first time they'd met. With only a little work on Silver's part, she was explaining the circumstances in which she'd disappeared from her parents' home. "I purchased the clothing secondhand, mostly, out of my own money. I said it was for charity."

"Your own money?"

"A legacy from my great-aunt," said Maud. "I knew any expedition would have to be well equipped." There was a bulky canvas backpack propped in a corner, next to the cleaver. "I ordered some things from the capital, and purchased others locally. Then it was a question of a suitable starting point. Do you know, I think it was your article on the Hallow Wood that put me onto it? I forget how you put it exactly, but you argued that any place long inhabited by the supernatural will in due course become supernatural in itself—didn't you?"

"Roughly," Silver agreed.

"Which struck me as back to front, rather," said Maud. "Would it not make just as much sense to say: any place supernatural in itself will in due course become inhabited by the supernatural?"

"The chicken-and-egg problem did occur to me, yes, but these things being so very hard to measure—"

"There being no reliable measurement for the incidence of magic," Maud agreed. "Or, for that matter, any way of measuring it."

"Precisely so. How on earth is one to know the, as it were, *ambient* power of a place without becoming familiar with its inhabitants?"

"Well, that's why I remembered the old Abbot," said Maud. "It seemed likely enough that a place where a vampire has lived for a thousand years probably has *some* magic lying about."

Silver coughed. For a moment, their dialogue had felt like a type of conversation he hadn't had in years, since before the Wood and before Tobias, even; the type of conversation one had with fellow learned young enthusiasts.

Which, it became increasingly clear, was what Maud was. She wanted to talk about magic; she wanted to talk about places of power; she wanted to talk about monsters—not what they were, but what they might *mean*. She was twenty-one years old and quite remarkably clever. She had read almost everything Silver had; God alone knew how she had got her hands on some of the more esoteric stuff. She had read some things

Silver hadn't; he had not been keeping up over the last year or two. She admitted freely to subscribing herself as a young man in letters to certain scholars she admired, the better to get some reasonable correspondence out of them. Silver let the conversation continue along byways marvellous and strange for some time. He found himself enjoying it. A creeping suspicion: had his self-indulgent wallowing at Greenhollow Hall (he could see, now, that it was self-indulgent) been as much boredom and loneliness as genuine misery?

"As a child, I had those books of fairy tales," said Maud. "You know the ones—all flowers and dewdrops. But when it becomes *real*—!" She leaned forward over her mug. Her watery blue eyes took on a surprising intensity; her voice was low and urgent. "Do you know what that's like—when the impossible becomes true right before your eyes?"

Silver *did* know, by God; he understood her perfectly. Tobias, as he had been: the Wild Man of Greenhollow, so solid and real that the rest of the world was dim by comparison. He swallowed.

"I remember the first time I understood what Abbot Julius really was," Maud said. "Oh, it was a little frightening, but how *extraordinary,* too. Nine centuries lay on his shoulders; sometimes you could see it in his eyes. Can you imagine that? To meet someone who had lived so long, and seen so much, and to *know* that you stood in the presence of magic—magic!"

"I can imagine," Silver said.

He knew very well the exact sensation Maud described, the thrill of discovery, the wonder of a living impossibility before one's eyes. Tobias sat now on what looked like an upturned gravestone, both hands around his mug of tea. He was only an ordinary man. The Hallow Wood had chosen another.

"And yet you killed the marvellous Abbot," he said.

"Yes; because I needed the crypt," said Maud. "Though also, he did eat people. If it hadn't been for that, I don't think I would have *killed* him."

"But, Miss Lindhurst—"

"Maud."

"—Maud. To bring us back to the point—why exactly *did* you need a place of supernatural significance to, as you put it, 'start from'? You mentioned an expedition?"

"Didn't I say?" said Maud, sounding quite surprised. "I'm going to Fairyland."

∼

Fairies.

Silver had been rather disappointed by fairies.

He had loved fairy tales as a boy, and he had read

widely as a young man. But fairies were conspicuously missing from the terse accounts, privately circulated, produced by practical folklorists like his mother. Where they appeared in the diaries Silver's father had kept as fuel for his researches, they were invariably noted with an *H* for hoax. *Local girl in costume. Paper cutouts and lantern. Petitioner deranged.*

Silver at fifteen had helped himself to his mother's keys and gone into the locked chest where she kept her own records of her most serious cases, but there had been no fairies there, either: just one incident of a missing child, where in her concluding notes Mrs Silver had written, *murdered undoubtedly, but little for a magistrate to go on; no evidence of fairy abduction as claimed; most likely the mother.*

And then he had discovered Tobias and the Wood—a real magical kingdom, a real spirit out of legends! And in the Lord of Summer he had been briefly convinced that he had found a fairy lord out of ancient ballads along with the rest. But there he had erred most seriously. Fabian Rafela, so-called Lord of Summer, had been another type of creature entirely.

There were a few petty-scholars among the hunters who passed their time in orderings and classifications. Silver's father had been among the best of them. About six months ago—well after Tobias's departure, this, as

Greenhollow Hall began to fall into an ivy-choked ruin—Silver had in a self-immolating mood gone through the lists and tables and concluded that Rafela had belonged among the *genii revocati malignantes*. He had spent an hour in the library then writing up a case note for the monster, in the style of his father's diaries: behaviour, intelligence, habitat, and prey.

He had not yet dared to investigate where he himself belonged in his father's tables. Presumably the Wood's avatar also came under the heading of spirits of place, the *genii locorum*.

Fairies had a whole collection of categories to themselves, with supposed classifications tentatively based on fairy tales and ballads. It was all speculation. Increasingly, sorrowfully, Silver had come to suspect they did not exist. But in the golden span of months where matters seemed to have resolved themselves rather well, he had asked Tobias about it. Lounging on Greenhollow's lawn over the remains of a picnic—Silver with a book, Tobias as ever with some small work of his hands to do, carving perhaps, or sewing, Silver could not recall it now—the question had occurred to him out of nowhere.

And Tobias had said, "Oh, them?"

Under his neatly trimmed beard, the corners of his mouth had turned down.

This was what the former Wild Man of Greenhollow

had to say about fairies:

They were real.

They did, indeed, take children—occasionally. They usually forgot to feed them.

He believed they were sensible beings, able to think and plan and converse, though he had never as a matter of fact heard one speak.

They were rare. Very rare. In his four hundred years in the Wood, Tobias had encountered no more than half a dozen for sure; though sometimes he thought they had passed through the Wood and he had not seen them.

"Not seen them?" Silver had asked. "Do you mean you couldn't find them? Or were they invisible?"

Tobias had thought about it. "Invisible, I'd say, after a fashion. They don't find it easy, I think, to be here."

"To be *here*? So they come from somewhere else?" Silver could not help grinning in his excitement. "From their own kingdom? From Fairyland?"

Tobias shrugged. "Who can say?"

"Surely *you* can, if anyone can at all."

"Never saw any sign of Fairyland," Tobias said. "Not a road, not a path. And as for a kingdom, well, I never saw a lord or a king, as you might call them. No, not a queen either," before Silver could say it. "Sometimes I'd feel a fairy loose in the Wood, but I couldn't find it. *You* know." Silver did know. The Wood was entirely open to

him, and he had learned that he could tell when something uncanny was afoot; could turn to Tobias and say, *I
believe the barrow on the eastern hill is waking up,* so Tobias
would nod and in his casual determined way set out by
night with pistol and flint knife to quiet a pack of flesh-
tearing ghouls.

"What do fairies feel like?" he'd asked. "When you feel
them."

Tobias had thought about it a little while.

"Old," he'd said at last. "Sad."

~

"Of course it exists," said Maud Lindhurst. The candlelight flickered on her tightly bound guinea-gold hair: the
paraffin stove gave off a faint glow that lit her long face
from below, making skull-shadows of her cheeks and
brows. "How could it not exist? Consider how many legends of Fairyland there are. No smoke without fire, you
know. A lady investigating our country's folklore may feel
as sure of the Kingdom of Fairy as a lady investigating
railway tracks may be sure of steam engines."

"I have thought as much myself," Silver admitted. By
God, how he had hungered for Fairyland once! The
Wood had taken up some of that space in his thoughts;
but what was the good of it, in the end? He had rejoiced

so greatly in his discoveries. Now his house was a ruin; he had no good clothes left; his main social intercourse was with a dryad who plainly thought him an inferior specimen of humanity, though Bramble would probably have regarded kings and emperors as inferior next to Tobias Finch.

Maybe he had forgotten himself, somewhere, between the Wood and Fabian Rafela and Tobias bloody Finch. If it took a girl like this to remind him what it had felt like to have a serious conversation about the supernatural, then it really had been too long. Who was he, if not Henry Silver, gentleman scholar, hunter of secrets, lover of fairy tales?

"God knows it would be a remarkable discovery," he said. "I don't deny it. Amazing—marvellous—if it were possible. But no one has ever found Fairyland yet, and you must know you're not the first to try. What makes you so sure you know where you're going?"

Maud was grinning. The expression lit up her awkward face. "It's simple enough. I've been there before," she said.

Through all this Tobias had sat in silence, like a man carved of wood. Silver had almost—almost—let himself ignore the man's presence. But at that he sucked in a breath.

Maud turned her head and gazed at Tobias in rudely direct curiosity for a long moment.

"It *is* you," she said. "I thought so all along. I was only a child, but I don't forget. Do you remember me? In your wood?"

And as she said it Silver realised with a lurching sensation that *he* actually had a kind of memory of her, a vision of a silent little yellow-haired scrap of humanity in the arms of a shimmering half-seen figure disappearing among the trees. It was his thought and yet *not* his thought. It came from the Wood.

"Yes, miss," said Tobias heavily. "I remember."

~

At the age of six Maud Lindhurst, visiting her aunt near Hallerton, had been kidnapped by a fairy.

She was not able to describe, exactly, what the fairy looked like. *Its legs were long,* she said. *Its eyes were hard to look at.*

It had taken her to a strange place along a road made of moonlight. She had been very hungry, but she had not made a sound. Being an intelligent and resourceful six-year-old, she had paid attention to the road; and when her peculiar captor's attention was distracted on their arrival, she had stood up on her small and sturdy legs and run back along the silver pathway until she found herself among *trees, lots of trees.*

There the fairy, rushing after her, had caught her again and picked her up in its arms; and she had looked into its disturbing eyes and it had said something, maybe, though Maud could not say what the words were or even if it had been speaking in a language she knew.

"What was it like?" asked Silver, fascinated. The candles on their tall golden candlesticks guttered and flickered, casting dancing shadows over the walls of Abbot Julius's crypt.

"Sad," said Maud, her expression very distant. "It was so sad."

Then, as the human child stared up at its captor and the fairy continued to—speak? To sing?—a big man in big boots had come stomping out of the woods towards them. The fairy had taken fright and tried to run, but the burden of a human child had been too much for it—Maud described it as skinny, spindly even, without strength in its long limbs—and it had carefully set her down on a grassy knoll. The big man had come upon her there, crying furiously, surrounded by a ring of white mushrooms. He had been very fearsome. When he tried to pick her up, Maud screamed and ran away; and strangely enough, the trees had moved around her, so that she found herself stumbling out of the straggling edge of Greenhollow Wood and into the outskirts of Hallerton village, where the aunt she was staying with had not even noticed she was missing.

Quiet followed Maud's story.

"I got there too late," Tobias said abruptly. "Always feared as much, when I saw it'd left you in a ring. You're mazed, miss; you're fairy-mad. Like a mouse that's looked a snake in the eye. Better go home to your parents."

Maud stared at him a moment in silent outrage and then turned to Silver. "Do I seem mad to you?" she demanded.

"You seem like a very unusual young lady," Silver said carefully.

"*Unusual!* And so you'll cart me home and send me to bed without my supper, will you? And then my parents will send me for rest cures, and cut off my correspondence, and take my books again, and—" She stood up. Her right hand was in the pocket of her corduroys: not a casual gesture, Silver understood perfectly well, because that was the pocket with the revolver in it. "Well, gentlemen, it has been terribly interesting to meet you. For a moment I thought at least one of you would understand. If you'll excuse me, I mean to chart the road to Fairyland, to discover its history and its society, and by interview and observation to ascertain the nature of its inhabitants. I know the way; I have walked it before. Good night."

She moved swiftly, swinging the canvas pack up onto

her shoulders, leaving the cleaver; she was halfway up the ladder Silver had barely noticed in the far corner of the room before either Silver or Tobias had time to react. Tobias moved first.

"She has a gun," Silver said behind him as they started up the ladder, "for God's sake, be careful—"

Tobias grunted in assent.

So this was what they were now: partners in a professional matter, hunters of the supernatural, rescuers of alarming young ladies. So this was what became of falling in love with a marvel out of legend.

Silver thought he might, in time, become resigned to it.

~

In the flickering firelit shadows of the vampire's lair, Silver had half-forgotten where they were. Emerging behind Tobias onto the hillside above Rothport, he took a great gasp of the cold sea air and felt tremendously grateful for it. Tobias put out a hand to steady him when he stumbled. It was an unthinking kindness, like passing a coin to the tramp. Silver could expect nothing from him, now, except the kindness that ran deep in his nature as the current of a rushing stream. But it was good to breathe freely again. The death-scent lingering underground had been mostly his imagination, he was sure. Mostly.

The ruined abbey's bones rose out of the earth about them, dark and slick with rain though the skies had cleared. Below them Rothport curled around the dark blot of the bay, its one string of gas lamps flaring like stars to mark the line of the high street. Silver could not see Maud at first. Then Tobias said sharply, "There!"

The girl was standing at the very edge of the cliff. Silver understood, with a sudden lurch, one way a child from a seaside town might make sense of a *shining road*. The moon above was high and full and very bright; and Maud's lanky figure swayed a little.

"Miss Lindhurst!" Silver cried, and then remembered. "Maud—wait!"

Tobias was a coiled spring at his side, readying himself to tackle her, which struck Silver as a very bad idea. Maud had gone still. Mazed, fairy-mad, whatever that meant; he felt a flicker of irritation—how many things must Tobias know that he had never yet mentioned?—but Silver schooled his face to calm and went a little closer.

When her figure stiffened he stopped. Tobias was lurking in his shadow. Silver prayed that he would have the sense not to interfere. From here he could see past the cliff's edge to the murmuring shadows below. By daylight it would be a beautiful sea view. The full moon was painting the caps of little waves with pale light. "You must be very sure of your road, Miss Lindhurst," Silver managed, with an approximation of good cheer.

Maud cast him an icy impatient look, just visible in the gloom. "I am," she said. Silver put out a hand towards Tobias to hold him back from any foolish heroics. Heaven alone knew what the footing was like. The odds were good that any man trying to grab Maud away from that deadly edge would only go over the cliff with her, and the two of them would be swallowed together by the water below—no, Silver recalled his glimpse of the bay that afternoon; the water gave way to stark black knife-edges of rock below the abbey.

His hand collided with Tobias's chest, nearer than he'd thought. Tobias was still in just his shirtsleeves; Silver could feel the warmth of him. And he could hear the big man's breathing, slow and measured; the breaths of a frightened man calming himself. *Not now,* he chided his own skittering thoughts, and snatched his hand away.

"Well?" said Maud.

Silver had not really had a plan after *wait.* He improvised. "I believe you were right," he said. About what? The girl clearly longed to be right; she had read Silver's father's work, she corresponded with experts under an assumed name— "About the chicken-and-egg problem," he said. "You were quite right."

Maud half-turned towards him, frowning. Little black

pebbles skidded away from under her feet.

"It *could* be that supernatural places give rise to magical beings, but it could just as easily be the case that the presence of a supernatural being effects a—a transformation of place," Silver said. He was making it up as he went along. "You must grant, therefore, that it is entirely possible that with the death of the, er, tenant, Rothling Abbey has already reverted to being an ordinary romantic ruin, rather than a place of power—"

"You won't stop me," said Maud.

"I only think," said Silver, "that you ought to have some insurance. What a waste of your plans and preparation it would be if you hurled yourself to an untimely death instead of onto your road just now, all because you lacked—"

He stopped.

Maud's long face and small mouth lent themselves well to sneering. "Lacked a suitably magical companion?"

The shape of what Silver had just talked himself into unfolded before him, alarming and wonderful. A scientific expedition to Fairyland; what an absurd, brilliant idea. It was just the sort of thing a former version of Henry Silver would have hurled himself into without a second thought. It was just the sort of thing he had always loved. And on that clifftop, with Tobias Finch big and solid and utterly untouchable standing a foot away, nothing waiting for him but the loneliness of Greenhollow, his ruined house, an angry dryad—*oh,* the joy Silver felt, all at once, at the thought of something positively mad to do.

"Yes," he said, and smiled at her, unforced. "May I offer myself?"

"*You,*" she said, with obvious disbelief. Her eyes flicked sideways to his companion.

"Mr Finch is what you might call a *retired* supernatural being," said Silver, feeling the words on his tongue coming light as quicksilver. "I, on the other hand—"

The Wood was not here on the height; this place had been wind-scoured for millennia. But as Silver very carefully took another pace towards Maud on the cliff edge, as he swallowed back a gulp of hysterical laughter, he thought of that drowned forest he had sensed earlier. It was there, just at the softening edge of the world, under the vast darkness of the ocean. Silver rather theatrically lifted a hand, and as he did, there was a change in the quality of the sound which murmured and murmured below the cliff. The wind soughed in the branches of trees that were not there. Maud had turned all the way towards him now, her eyes wide, and Silver smiled at her and plucked from the creeper that had just twined its way up the ruined black wall closest to him a handful of pink and white blossoms. He held it out to the girl.

With a rather good charming air—if he said so himself—he added, "You read my article, I believe you said."

"The Hallow Wood," said Maud. She looked at the posy of flowers uncertainly, and then met Silver's eyes. Her slim shoulders squared.

"My name first," she said. "When we publish. This is my expedition."

"Alphabetically, of course," said Silver. "It's a privilege even to be invited, Miss Lindhurst." And before she could correct him, he corrected himself: "Maud." He was still awkwardly holding the posy. Maud had not taken it. He tossed it carelessly aside as he added, "I hope you will consider me in the light of a brother—a brother in scholarly inquiry, if nothing else."

After a long pause Maud said, "Very well."

Silver took another step closer. There was now so little distance between them that he could offer her his arm. The black pebbles were falling away into darkness under his feet as well as hers. Behind them the ruins of the abbey were rain-slick, shining faintly under the moon; and as Silver glanced back, he saw Tobias bend and pick up the silly little posy of pink and white flowers. They looked small and foolish in his big hands, and they were wilting already. It was too dark to make out Tobias's expression. Not that it mattered, because the days when Silver had exerted his utmost powers to decoding Tobias's small changes of expression, his rare frowns, his rarer smiles—those days were over. An expedition to Fairyland, Silver told himself; an opportunity, a delight. Something mad and wonderful to do, because the world was not devoid of marvels after all.

Maud's right hand settled carefully on Silver's left forearm.

That meant her right hand was an instant or two further away from the damn revolver in her pocket.

This was the moment when Silver had intended to use what little force he could bring to bear—he was not a Tobias Finch, but for all her height, Maud was a slim young woman—to drag her backwards while she least expected it. This was the moment he had meant to remind himself and Tobias and his bloody mother too that he was *not* a nonentity and not a fool either. He had let the picture lurk quietly under the surface of his thoughts, knowing very well that the best way to tell a lie was to believe it entirely in the moment, but it had been there: Miss Lindhurst escorted safely home, to grieving mother and pompous father. Tobias impressed. Mrs Silver impressed. After which Silver himself would—would turn to Tobias and say with a charming air—

No, turn his *back* to Tobias and remark lightly to his mother—

No, no: return to his ruined manor house, and perhaps

say something witty and intelligent to—

To whom? To *Bramble*?

He was missing the moment. Already Maud was furrowing her brows as she took in his expression, and he was a man standing on a cliff above the ocean on the edge of a deadly fall onto razor rocks, arm in arm with a girl with more courage than sense. Tobias was looking on with Heaven alone knew what expression in the dark, and the moon was shining on the water, and there was a soft sighing of the wind, rustling in the leaves of a drowned forest, filling all the air.

And then, with a sense that did not belong to an ordinary mortal, Silver was aware of something bent and strange in that chilly murmuring air; as if the night were doubled over on itself, and a hole torn through it.

"Good God," he said, "there really is a road."

Maud stiffened. Silver grabbed ahold of her hand before she drew it away entirely. "I'm sorry! I shouldn't have doubted you. Don't— You need me, I swear you do." It was true; it was the Wood that was calling that strange path into being. He was sure of it; he could feel it. But he needed her as well. Something marvellous had left its mark on her, and it was at her feet that the shining road began. "Your name first," he reminded her. "When we publish."

Maud's lips pressed tight together. "My name first," she

agreed, and hoisted her canvas pack a little more firmly on her shoulders.

"Silver!"

Tobias's voice was hoarse. Silver had somehow, for the first time since he had come to Rothport, genuinely forgotten that he was there. He turned now to give Tobias a brilliant smile, unforced, uncalculated, entirely sincere. It was not that it no longer hurt to look at him. The queer ache endured, as it had continuously from the moment he'd set eyes on Tobias again and found him larger than memory, sterner and kinder and more ordinary and entirely himself. By God, how Silver had loved the man! He had loved him to the tune of fourteen months spent pitying himself in a thorn-girt fortress. But there was no use dwelling now: Silver was even able to admit to himself, here, at last, that the whole mess had in the end been entirely and predictably his own fault.

"Once again, my dear sir," he said, "I am going to have to ask you to explain matters to my mother."

Perhaps he should not have made a joke of it. The last time Silver had asked him that favour, he had been on the point of getting eaten alive by an ancient and evil parasite power in the beautiful, appalling form of Fabian Rafela.

Oh well. It didn't matter now.

Silver stepped off the cliff and onto the road to Fairyland. Maud came with him. She was clinging to his arm a little, though her expression was set. Fearless, yes: but she had not been totally oblivious to the potential of those dreadful knife-edged rocks.

"Silver, for God's sake!"

Tobias moved fast for such a big man. But the road was not there for him, and the edge of the Rothling headland was less forgiving of his heavy tread than it had been of slim Maud and light-footed Silver. Not pebbles but whole clods of earth skidded away from under his boots. Silver saw it happen, saw his balance fail, saw him begin to fall.

No, he thought or said; and Time itself shifted around him in answer.

Down they went all together, Maud with a shrill cry and Tobias with a shout and Silver himself concentrating too hard to make a sound. Down they went, breaking branches of protesting trees as they went, gathering bruises and cuts aplenty; down to a half-forgiving landing in a dim and wild wood that had vanished under the rising waves ten thousand years before.

II

The Fairy Queen

TWO YEARS AGO

ON A MARCH MORNING around dawn, after a night of honest conversation—*conversation,* with Tobias Finch!—Silver made a joke, and Tobias blinked once and put his big hand on Silver's jaw and kissed him.

What a shock it was, after months of flirtation that might as well have been aimed at an amiable wall. What an astounding, delightful shock, to find oneself sincerely admired, and wanted, and *liked*—and by such a sober and immovable rock of a man as Tobias Finch!

March was casting off her chills; the twigs of the hawthorn budding; the bluebells coming into carpeting bloom as spring breathed out over the wood. Silver, enchanted, even found himself in charity with his mother. She was pleased to see him well, she said; and in that stiff little sentence he heard more human feeling than he had ever known her to express before. Her eyes were wet, and she dabbed at them aggressively with a handkerchief, as if daring him to say anything. Silver, quite overcome, embraced her. When she squawked in surprise, he laughed. The laughter rolled up out of him like the bubbles of the rushing Haller Brook.

(Later Silver wondered if the air of spring had been a part of it. Perhaps he had been drunk on the season. Perhaps he should never have expected such a budding green joyfulness to last.)

Mrs Silver lingered at Greenhollow Hall for most of a month, and Silver only fought with her twice. Both times they cut themselves off before the squabble could really get going; both times they each glanced at Tobias, big and quiet and trying not to look unhappy, and thought the better of their disagreement. Silver's mother *liked* Tobias. Silver had never seen her like anyone half so much. She liked his solidness, she liked his practicality, she liked his tidy habits and his gruff manners and his excellent aim with a pistol. "I am so very pleased," she said to Silver once, "that you seem to have developed some good sense in your personal affairs at last."

This was by far the most approving thing Mrs Silver had ever said about any of Silver's entanglements. She had an eagle eye for spotting them, and a scathing tongue for the failings of each. In the high good humour that possessed him near every moment of that glorious spring, Silver grinned at her and said, "I admit, madam, that I have done much worse."

"Hmph!" said Mrs Silver.

A week later she departed. It was almost May; bumblebees bumped and rolled through the air around the lavender bushes like drunken sailors, and Mrs Silver had her own business to attend to. She announced it briskly at dinner on a Tuesday night and was gone by Thursday morning.

"I'll tarry a while yet," Tobias said the night before she went. He sat on the edge of the bed and passed Silver a cup of water. His manner was abrupt. Silver realised, delighted, that he was being shy.

But it was only then that it occurred to him, for the first time, that Tobias might leave.

"My dear fellow," Silver said, trying not to sound panicked, "more than a while, surely. You cannot mean to leave me to Bramble's tender mercies." He forced anxiety out of his expression and stretched out, luxurious, smiling, on the white bedsheets. "It's odd—I thought she liked me—but she seems to have grown less approving of late. Do you think she might be jealous?"

Tobias ducked his head. "Foolishness," he muttered, but there was a smile lurking on his face.

"In her position," Silver said, with growing relief, "I would certainly be jealous." There, let him forget about it. Tobias enjoyed being teased; Silver was happy to tease him.

But Tobias shook his head. "I'll tarry a while," he repeated. "For the summer, maybe."

"Tobias," Silver said, sitting up, more serious as he perceived that Tobias really meant it, "Greenhollow has been your home much longer than it has been mine. I cannot perceive any reason you should ever leave." He brushed his hand over the swell of Tobias's bare arm. "Not now."

"She's not young," Tobias said, "your mother. It's a dangerous business she's in. And she pays me a wage."

"My mother is immortal," said Silver, "probably. I would wager on her over a hurricane. And she has been managing her dangerous business alone without the slightest difficulty since I was five years old. Tobias, she doesn't *need* you. Ask her as much—she'll say the same—and for heaven's sake, my dear, don't think of *money*—"

He took a handful of Tobias's shaggy hair to claim him for a kiss. Tobias allowed it; was smiling a little into it. He almost always let Silver have his way. And why should he leave, anyway? To run Mrs Silver's errands? To carry her luggage? If he wanted to hunt monsters, let him do it here, in the wood, Silver's wood. Here was the heart of Silver's domain; here the glade where the aspen trees grew, here the earth which had covered him. Silver could perhaps follow Tobias wherever he went, so long as the Wood had been there once; but the prospect of that much time spent in his *mother's* company—not that it wasn't convenient that she liked Tobias, but must Tobias also like *her*?

Silver woke with the birdsong, well before Tobias did. Tobias had confided that it was strange to him being able to sleep through the dawn. It was bloody strange for Silver *not* being able to sleep through it. After a lifetime of regarding the sun as a cruel tyrant attempting to prevent him from reading as late as he wanted to at night and sleeping as late as he wanted to in the morning, his newmade body suddenly found the first light of morning irresistible.

He brushed his hair and tied it back, and laughed at the scatter of leaf-mould left on his comb. Somehow it kept being surprising, the way the Wood was woven all through him. Then he threw on the tweed jacket Tobias had left on the back of a chair and went out for a walk through the dewdropped wildland under the glow of the morning sky.

He took himself down to the aspen glade, there to politely greet the four queen dryads in whom, obscurely, he felt his dominion over the Wood resided. They swayed and rustled in the breeze, their leaves shimmering between green and gold; fat fluffy catkins were shaking off their first thick drifts of pollen. Silver sneezed, more out of habit than because he really needed to. As he ambled back towards his house, he felt Bramble in the trees about him. "Good morning!" he said.

She faded into view for a moment among the bracken. Spring had given her a crown of white blossom. She was frowning. Silver on impulse kissed his hand to her.

"Don't worry," he said. "I won't let him leave."

NOW

"Where are we?" said Maud.

"The Hallow Wood," said Silver, and at the same time Tobias said, "The wood, miss."

They exchanged glances. The wind whispered in the trees around them with a sound like the sighing of an ocean.

"We're nowhere near Greenhollow," objected Maud.

"If you read my monograph," Silver retorted, "then you should know that the Hallow Wood is considerably larger—and older—than any individual fragment."

"Your monograph was a great many words used to say hardly anything—"

"For God's sake, Miss Lindhurst, is this the *time*?"

"Don't patronise me!"

Tobias's hand came down heavy and solid on Silver's shoulder before he could say the several unpleasant things that occurred to him. "Seems to me it's my fault," he said quietly, "if it's anyone's, miss; but we know our business, Mr Silver and I. There's nothing to fear."

"I'm not *afraid*!" Maud said.

Tobias went over to her. He wordlessly took the pack she carried and hoisted it onto his own shoulders without effort. Supplies for one woman, to go between three of them, one Tobias's size. Silver probably didn't need food to stay alive, but he did not relish the thought of finding out.

"As Mr Finch says," he said, "there's nothing to fear." Time was soft here, blurring the landscape at the edges of his vision; Silver was working hard to *keep* it soft, since he had a dreadful feeling that if he let the two mortals slip back into their proper place in the order of things, they would promptly be drowned under the black ocean which had claimed this place. He had wandered far, first in curiosity and then in a maudlin half-desire to get lost and never come back, but this piece of the Wood was like nothing else he had ever felt. The trees stood straight and strong, old beech and elm. An odd half-light that came from no sun penetrated their canopy and dappled the forest floor. They were green with the foliage of an unending summer that had endured, suspended between one instant and the next, for millennia. Nothing else alive was here. Silver knew it as assuredly as he knew that he had five fingers on each hand.

He swallowed down his terror and his awe. "It's going to be a rather stiff walk, I'm afraid," he said. "And mostly uphill. But we should be back in Rothport soon enough." He hoped.

Tobias set the pack a little firmer across his back and nodded.

"*No*," said Maud. "I'm not going back. Give me back my things." She pulled the revolver out of her pocket but did not point it at either of them—not yet. "I'm going to Fairyland, with you or without you," she said. "The road is—"

She stopped.

Silver didn't say anything. The sense he'd had on the Rothport cliff of something bent double in the air was gone. This place was still and empty and devoid of all paths.

"No," said Maud. "No! I was so *close*!"

She gestured wildly with the hand that had the revolver in it. Silver winced. Tobias took several silent steps back from her. "Now, miss," he said, soft and firm, just as he might have spoken to calm an enraged dryad. "Listen—"

No dryad, Maud.

"You!" she spat. "If you hadn't interfered—again!" She pointed the revolver at Tobias. Her expression was wild but her hand was damnably steady. Silver's heart lurched in alarm. He opened his five-fingered human hands and spoke. He said, unthinkingly, a word in a language he had never learned. He called.

And something came.

It was something living, something wild, something old. It came charging out of the trees in a headlong rush. Silver got a glimpse of hairy flank and a strong scent of rank flesh, and thought: *A goat?* It dashed between Maud and Tobias, knocking them apart and knocking Maud flat on her back. The revolver fell out of her hand and she let out a startled cry. The beast turned, sending up sprays of dry earth around its hooves, and charged with heavy tread back towards the prone girl; it would trample her to death, and Silver could only stare, thinking at once, *She meant to kill* and *I did not mean to kill—*

But the goat-beast never reached Maud again. Tobias, swift as the wind and immovable as a rock, had planted himself in its path. The beast charged towards him and bounced off his strong shoulder, braced hard against it. He let out an *oof* but did not budge.

The creature turned. It was hard to get a good look

at the thing: the moonless moonlight of this in-between place sidled away from it, only getting caught here and there in clumps of matted fur. But by God, the smell! It was looking at Silver. Silver looked back. He stared into its mad, slit-pupiled golden eyes and thought, *Oh God, what have I done.*

"Silver!" yelled Tobias. "Climb a goddamn tree!"

The goat-beast let out a shrill screech and hurled itself towards him.

Were there hooves? Horns? It had eyes, Silver knew: did it have a suggestion of a face? He could hear Maud on the ground laughing with a hysterical breathless sound, near sobs. This was his fault. He had been afraid and had done what seemed natural, and now this was his fault, and by God, the thing *was* running straight at him—

He did not know what to do.

He did some magic.

He held out his hand and there was an apple in it: small, sour, wizened. The goat-beast came lolloping towards him with a great squealing and a dreadful waft of that rank meat smell. Silver weighed the apple in his hand, waited until he judged the thing was near enough, and then hurled the fruit square at it with his best schoolboy overarm.

It went through the thing's flesh. The beast was not quite *here;* Silver felt the un-hereness of it the same way he felt the un-hereness of the long-drowned trees. But the apple was as real and solid as Silver's boots. It lodged in the goat-beast's half-real heart, and Silver licked his lips and spoke again in that language he had never learned. The words came to him out of the same strand of memory that had known Maud for a child once lost in the woods; a memory that was older than he was, and older than Tobias too.

The apple erupted: stick and stem and root and bough, the growth of generations unfurling in all directions. The goat-beast squealed in an unpleasantly human voice that cut off in a gargle as a branch rammed its seeking way out of its throat. The tree was pinning it into the moment; its moon-silvered mats of fur were gaining density and texture, and that *was* a human face, set above shaggy-furred but human shoulders; and the forearms ended in square and powerful hands, though the hind legs were tipped with hooves.

"A satyr," Silver whispered aloud, fascinated despite the horror of it. The creature's corpse was bleeding where branches perforated it. Its eyes were wide and staring and filming over in death. It was very, very dead. He swallowed.

The apple tree came into flower as he flexed the fingers of his left hand, his throwing hand; and the flowers fell as he let out a breath. They made a white carpet on the dim ground as the fruit began to blush on the branch in dull red clusters.

Silver felt Tobias's eyes on him as a physical weight. His stomach was squirming.

He walked slowly towards the gnarled, bloody mass of tree and corpse. It was more of a hobble than a walk. His limbs were aching through and through, as if he had spent his energy in some great physical exertion. Maud was scrambling to her feet, staring at him. There was a long bruise on the side of her face.

The satyr smelled just as rank in death as it had living. Gore dripped from every place where the tree's growing had speared it. Its ribcage and gut were open wide. Blood and viscera fouled the bark. The tree was unperturbed. Silver, dreamlike, watched his own hand reach for a dark apple and twist it off the bough.

"*Surely* you've read *something* of the dangers of fairy fruit," said Maud, with a remarkable if shaky attempt at her usual briskness, just as Silver was about to take a bite.

And Silver hesitated: and Tobias was there, suddenly, at his right hand. He plucked the apple out of Silver's limp fingers and threw it away into the shadows under the trees. Silver stared stupidly at him. Tobias had Maud's revolver in his hands now. When had he picked it up? He took the shot out of it and scattered the powder, and then it went into another pocket.

"I didn't really mean—" Maud said.

"If you didn't mean to shoot, Miss Maud," said Tobias, "you shouldn't have taken aim." He turned his frown on Silver. "And *you* ought to know better than to play the fool with old gods' matters."

"Is that what I did?"

Tobias jerked his chin at the satyr and the apple tree. "Don't know what else you'd call that."

"Well, I—the Wood—"

"I know the wood," Tobias said firmly. "Four hundred years I knew the wood. But I never made myself a bloody wizard on the back of it. That's Fay's business. Bad business. You should know better."

Fay was the dead Fabian: a pet name, Silver had once worked out, with not a little jealousy. Perhaps it was the sting of that jealousy now which led him to say quite coldly, "Mr Finch, I don't believe our acquaintance as it stands justifies so much familiarity on your part. The Wood and I are not your concern."

As a withering setdown this failed entirely. Tobias took it in stride with only a slightly quirked eyebrow—was that disapproval? Amusement? It was so hard to know—and turned back to Maud. "What did he say to you?" he said. "Your elf."

Maud looked away. "Why does it matter?"

"You're fairy-mad for sure. You'd do better to go home

and forget. But since you won't"—Tobias's voice held a grim note Silver had never heard—"we'd better see the business through."

"I don't know," said Maud. "I don't know what he said. I told you, I can't remember. I was only a little girl. What does it matter?" Her voice rose. "*You* interfered—and *he* interfered—and we're lost, lost, the road is gone, and I've *failed*—"

"Ah," said Silver. "About that."

All this time the gore had been dripping down the apple tree, soaking the earth among the roots and remnants of hooves until it turned dark and sodden and began to puddle. In the shine of that gory pool, Silver could feel the twist of the air that marked Maud's road.

He said, "I believe it's just through here."

As he spoke, the trees of the drowned forest shimmered and faded from view like a mist. They were still there: Silver could feel them. But they were also *not* there; or rather Silver himself, and Tobias and Maud, were somewhere else. Could the others even feel the strangeness of it, these two places superimposed one over the other? It made Silver's teeth ache faintly somewhere near the back of his mouth.

The horizon opened out wide and pale: a pinkish sky illuminating black earth with rosy light. There were no trees in this place save the apple tree that pinioned the satyr. It was now in full fruit with big round apples that gleamed a poisonous scarlet. The rotten stink of the satyr was overpoweringly thick in the air.

"Oh," breathed Maud.

"Hm," Tobias said.

"What?" said Silver. He really thought Tobias could have been at least a *little* impressed.

"So that's Fairyland," said Tobias. He shrugged. "Nasty place."

TWO YEARS AGO

Tobias stayed, through May, through June. Midsummer came and went and no dark power rose in the woods; the Lord of Summer was dead as could be. Silver had known it already, but he caught a little of Tobias's edginess all the same and kept close by him all that day and all that night.

The Lord of Summer was dead; Fabian Rafela, who had by some evil wizardry bound himself to that ancient spirit, was also dead; only the Wood lived, and Silver lived as its avatar. He went down to the aspen glade a day or two after the solstice to check on the rubbled ruins of the dead god's altar. Very little of that ancient structure was left on the surface; he could feel broken stone under the earth. There was no life in it; it would not rise again. The aspen trees shivered in the breeze. Their dryads were silent.

Truth be told, it was Rafela who concerned Silver, not the monster he'd become. Fabian Rafela in life had been an evil man, but he had been a *man;* nor did Silver think he had ever intended to become merely the crooked mask of an inhuman power. Perhaps he had lost some struggle early on with the demon he'd bargained with. But as Silver wrote up his monograph on the Hallow Wood, and interviewed some more locals about the Wild Man legend for the look of the thing, and ordered books for his library, and kept his lover good company all through the summer, he felt as if he were only going through the motions of what Henry Silver would do. He was something else now, something old, something strange.

It frightened him.

What frightened him more was his suspicion that he would go on growing older and stranger every year that passed. The mask of Henry Silver would fall further and further away with the centuries, and maybe he would forget his beautiful house with its beautiful library and end up wandering enchanted eternally in his wood. *Tobias* had kept the timelessness of immortality at bay with countless invented chores: with building and maintain-

ing his little cottage, hunting the monsters that Greenhollow bred, preparing grimly year after year for midsummer: and on top of that he'd always kept a cat. He
indulged the tabby Pearl still, though she was, as far as
Silver could tell, entirely self-sufficient on squirrels and
sparrows and had no need whatsoever for Tobias to save
her fish from his supper.

Tobias, it had to be admitted, had very little imagination. Silver was unfortunately cursed with a good one.

Immortality stretched bleakly ahead of him, immortality and the Wood. How would it be when his mother
was gone, when Tobias was gone—when not only spoilt
Pearl but all the lines of her feline descendants had spent
themselves? Even dryads, bound to their trees, did not
endure forever. Silver looked out on the prospect of millennia and thought: *Perhaps the thing that called itself the
Lord of Summer started as a mortal man as well.*

More than once he thought of bringing the question
up with Tobias, but what could Tobias even say? He had
given his advice already: he had told Silver to keep a cat,
and it would keep him awake. At some point in July, Pearl
produced six kittens. Silver liked cats perfectly well, but
he could not imagine finding one interesting enough that
it would bind him to humanity.

NOW

Fairyland was empty.

There was no living thing, nor any sign one had ever been there. There was no bird or bee or crawling insect, no breath of air, not a single weed—not so much as a dandelion. And there were no graceful winged beings dressed in flower petals like the ones Silver had liked in the illustrations from his childhood books of fairy tales, no lords and ladies adorned in dew and starlight: only this flat empty land. In Silver's perception it clung on to the edges of the drowned Wood like fog clings to earth. Black standing stones were all that relieved the emptiness: dull guardsmen keeping watch over a dead land.

Tobias was stone-faced as ever, but Silver thought he could spot the outlines of *I told you so* in his expression.

"There must be someone here. Smoke and fire," said Maud. Her stubborn little mouth was a flat line. "There *must* be someone." She looked around as if the fairy she had met long ago might appear suddenly, as if she had expected it to be waiting for her.

There was no one. Black earth and a pink sky; an apple tree all poisonous bright; the stench of rotten meat; and in every direction flat empty land, broken up only by scattered upright stones arranged in discomfiting patterns which almost, almost, suggested a grand design. Silver had a dreadful feeling the monoliths were moving when he was not looking. He had no idea why this should fill him with anxiety, but it did.

"Perhaps we had better explore a little," he said.

"Better stay away from those things," Tobias said, nodding to the nearest monolith: a monstrous black heap of rock, twice as tall as he was, alarmingly spindly at the base.

"We are looking for people, Mr Finch," Silver reminded him. "We are unlikely to find them by heading in the opposite direction from the works of their hands."

"Hm," Tobias said, but he did not protest again.

So they walked. And they walked, and they walked, among the black upright stones, under that pinkish sky. The light never changed, though it seemed like they had been at it for hours. They only stopped when Tobias glanced around at the two of them and called a halt. Silver was still exhausted by whatever it was he had done to summon that satyr, and he felt as if his legs had turned to pig iron from all this bold striding across the empty land. Maud looked wilted and miserable, her bright hair coming loose in wisps from its stern coil.

Tobias, of course, looked like he could keep going for another million years, and he was the one carrying Maud's pack. Silver had never resented his air of solid capability quite so much before.

"Let's see what we've got to go on, then," Tobias said, and set the pack down.

It turned out that Maud had planned her scientific expedition to Fairyland in much the way Silver would have done in her shoes: allowing of course for the disadvantages she had faced in the form of inconvenient parents and unhelpful tradesmen. She had dried meat in paper packets, and hard dry biscuits, and a good portion of the weight of her pack proved to be bottles of Mr Flower's Patented Lemon Juice, Healthfulness Guaranteed, which struck Silver as sensible in a mad sort of way. She had her small kettle for boiling water, and she had three changes of men's clothes, and she had eight blank notebooks, pen and ink aplenty, and an abridged edition of the latest Encyclopaedia in three handsome leather-bound volumes.

"No tent," said Tobias.

"We'll find shelter with the inhabitants," Maud said.

Tobias's expression didn't change. Silver winced. He wouldn't have thought of a tent either.

"I am sure we shall find the locals sooner rather than later," he said, pretending confidence. The dizzyingly confusing patterns of monoliths had shown no sign of giving way to anything resembling civilisation as he understood it. Worse, the sense of the Wood in the back of Silver's mind insisted that they had not in fact moved at all from where they started. He had a feeling that if he turned around quickly enough, he would catch the blood-soaked apple tree sidling out of the corner of his vision, when it should have been at least a couple of miles away by now.

There was no water to boil in the little kettle, and no fuel for a fire. The expensive portable paraffin stove was still sitting in the crypt of Rothling Abbey with the cold remnants of their tin mugs of tea around it. They drank Mr Flower's Patented Lemon Juice. Silver had never tasted anything so sour in his life. Then they ate a hard biscuit apiece.

"No water, nothing to hunt," Tobias observed when they were done. He did not elaborate on the observation. He did not need to.

Maud only answered, "They're here. They must be. They *must* be."

Silver coughed. "May I suggest," he said, "a compromise?"

Maud took on the expression of a woman uninterested in compromises. Silver knew it well; it reminded him of his mother.

"I shan't try to patronise you," he said. "You are clearly too intelligent and well read to be fooled by flattery." There, some flattery to help things along. "As Mr Finch points out, however, we are ill supplied for three. It is not merely a question of wishing to find inhabitants; we *must* find inhabitants, or we shall be in a rather sticky situation before too long. Would you agree?"

"I suppose," Maud said.

"So, if no inhabitants appear," Silver said, "would you be opposed to returning home, resupplying with a more substantial expedition in view, and trying again at a later date?"

"You don't understand," Maud said quietly. "They *will* take my books. They won't let me out of their sight. They think it's foolishness—or that I'm mad—like *he* thinks I'm mad." Tobias did not react. He was occupied in repacking Maud's supplies according to some logic of his own. Maybe he hadn't heard. "And I suppose you think I'm mad too, really."

"A few years ago," Silver said, "I found something magical. Something extraordinary, in fact. And I simply knew that I had to understand everything about it, that I had to embrace it and call it my own. Someone much older and wiser than I was warned me to be careful."

"Were you?"

"No," Silver said. Tobias had expected the Lord of Summer to consume him, had warned Silver to stay away; and instead he had handed himself over to be consumed. He hadn't known what he was getting into. It was sheer luck he had survived; luck, and Tobias, and his mother.

"Do you regret it?"

"No," Silver said. "And I don't think you're mad. On the contrary. I think we are two of a kind."

"I *won't* go home," Maud said.

"Perhaps you'd like to visit Greenhollow Hall," Silver said. "I can introduce you to the dryads."

"Really?"

She was of an age to be his sister, and she was bright and determined and curious to the point of folly, and Bramble would probably like her more than she liked Silver—certainly she could not like her less. "Of course," Silver said. "Why not?"

Maud looked at him carefully and then said, "Very well. We hunt for the inhabitants a little longer. And if we find nothing, we turn back, and try again another time."

"Agreed," Silver said, and did not ask Tobias for his opinion. He did not even look over towards him. He was proud of himself for that.

TWO YEARS AGO

August. Long muggy days broken by thunderstorms. Tobias had not left yet. They went for long walks in the afternoon, under the cooling canopy of the trees, and came back late to eat bread and cheese for supper and keep one another company in whatever way seemed best to them.

Tobias could not read, but he liked to be read to. The subject matter did not matter much; he listened with equal satisfaction to news sheets and novels, the dry prose of academics and the sublime poetry of the great playwrights. Silver had picked out the plays thinking that maybe Tobias would know some of them; they were more or less of his time, after all. But Tobias shook his head, though once he corrected Silver's pronunciation of a line spoken by one of the clown characters, turning it into a pun that Silver had missed entirely.

Mostly, though, he listened in silence. Sometimes he closed his eyes. "My dear, I don't believe you're taking in a word I'm saying," Silver said one night.

Tobias shook his head. After a moment he confessed, "It's not the words, so much."

"Oh?"

"I like to hear you talk," Tobias said. "Your voice. Always did."

"Should I recite my multiplication tables?" Silver said, delighted. "There's a dictionary about here somewhere—I could read you that—"

Tobias snorted. But after a moment he said, a little carefully, as if he thought he might be saying something wrong, "Saw you had a letter."

"Oh—yes," Silver said. It had arrived that morning, from his mother. She had dealt with a "substantial haunting" since her last communication. As usual, she'd left out every detail Silver might have found interesting—what manner of ghost? When was it seen, and by whom? Had she managed to speak with it? Had it seemed an intelligent being, as traditional accounts held, or was it more like an echo, as some Continental theorists presently supposed?

Adela Silver, to all these and more: *A great deal of fuss over a benign manifestation that might as well have been left alone, & a rather dirty affair in the end owing to gravedigging &c. Some tiresome difficulties over payment also.*

"Not very interesting reading material, I'm afraid," he said. "My mother has never been the most sparkling correspondent."

"She's well, though," Tobias said.

"Oh, in the pink, I assure you. Working: nothing makes her happier."

"She mention—"

"Your name? No, not this time; you needn't hurry away yet. I hope you're not in a rush to abandon me."

"No," Tobias said. "Only—"

"Yes?"

"It's a funny thing," Tobias said. "Seems like I always had plenty to do, those days." Living as a hermit in the woods, he meant. "Now . . ."

The silence stood between them for a moment. "Tobias," Silver managed, rushing to fill it, "you can do anything you like; surely you know that." He stood up; he held out his hands. "And perhaps you would like—"

Tobias took him up on the invitation with a clear, shy pleasure, as he always did. They retired to the ground-floor bedroom. It was an unlikely lovers' bower, even with honeysuckle round the windows, but Silver did his best to thoroughly distract them both.

He burned his mother's letter the next morning, feeding it carefully to the fireplace in the library. The sight of Mrs Silver's stern handwriting crumbling to ash gave him a dreadful feeling of relief.

I am now bound to the fens on a case regarding a bridge troll, if my correspondent is to be believed. Let Mr Finch know that I would be very grateful for the resumption of his assistance as soon as practicable, both in matters requiring a shovel and in those delicate affairs where his substantial presence inspires promptitude and honest dealing in those to whom it does not come naturally. Your loving MOTHER—

But she didn't need Tobias. *Silver* needed him. He did. How old was the man—thirty, thirty-five? It was hard to know, and Tobias himself was vague about it.

But in any case Silver had fifty years if he was lucky. He did not intend to waste them.

NOW

Since they had halted for the time being anyway, Silver went to inspect one of the black monoliths. He took one of Maud's blank notebooks with him and attempted a sketch of some strange markings he found near the base. It was not his best work. He considered calling Tobias over to assist, thinking of those sketches he'd done of Rothport's vampire. But then they would have been trapped in conversation at close quarters, when Silver had been doing his absolute best for hours now to keep Maud as a buffer between them.

He did the best he could; he was better than his mother at this sort of thing, at least. Then for good measure he turned the notebook sideways and doodled the flat land, the wide horizon, the monoliths. He lacked the tools to attempt a map, but something in him was slowly sparking to life at the possibility. Imagine—a map of Fairyland!

When they came back, of course. They would have to come back. He was reaching for a future of sorts. Maud was young; she would live a good long while. Fairyland was a project that might absorb him for years—decades. *You cannot adopt an angry young lady like a stray cat,* a voice rather like his mother's said in his head. Silver suspected it of being his conscience. He shoved it to one side.

He had three more sketches, one of them quite good, by the time he returned to the others. Tobias had found thread and needle in Maud's belongings and was sewing something or other. If you dropped Tobias on a desert island in the middle of the ocean, Silver reflected, you would come back six months later to find he'd built a neat cottage out of driftwood and supplied it with curtains and bed linen woven entirely from—coconut hair, or something. There was no end to the man's quiet industriousness.

"Should we carry on?" Silver said.

"Let her rest," said Tobias, not looking up.

It was the first thing he'd said in a while. When he spoke his voice was always deeper and softer than one expected, his accent always a little startling in its oddness. Silver startled at it now. He had not realised Maud was asleep. But she was, curled up with Tobias's coat over her.

"You're a thing apart," Tobias went on, and now he *did* look up, "and I'm a tough old pack mule. But she's only a mortal girl, and it was close on dawn when we went over that cliff."

"Mr Finch," said Silver, "perhaps—now we have a moment—we should clear the air a little."

"There's naught to clear."

"I only wanted to say—"

"You're sorry?" Tobias said.

Yes, of course, was on the tip of Silver's tongue, *terribly sorry; I very much regret—I can only apologise—*

Tobias's eyes were hazel-green and serious. Silver stumbled over the lies. He *wasn't* sorry, not in the least, only—

"You're sorry you got caught," Tobias concluded, correctly. His mouth was very slightly turned down. Silver felt a sliver of unfamiliar shame. But Tobias shook his head. "No need to make a fuss. Done is done. There." He'd been sewing up a seam in the canvas pack. "Jammed full of books and bottles," he added, with another head-shake, this one amused.

Silver stood where he was, reaching without hope for words. Tobias had always liked to hear him talk. There had to be, somewhere, a combination of words both true and effective. There had to be *something* he could say that was both *I loved you, I love you, doesn't that damned well matter?* and also *So what if I lied, so what if I was selfish—what is love if not selfish—so what if I needed you—I still need you—and really, really, Mr Finch, shouldn't you be the one who's sorry? Aren't you the one who left me?*

TWO YEARS AGO

September brought the year's turning, and Silver's summer kingdom came crashing down.

He'd been awake with the dawn as he always was, and he'd left Tobias sleeping. Crab apples were swelling on the boughs of the crooked tree near the wood's boundary; Silver plucked one and bit into it. It was very sour, a month or so away from ripe. Silver dropped the bitten apple into the pocket of Tobias's tweed jacket, which he'd stolen off the back of the chair in their bedroom, and went looking for Bramble. He had not seen her in some time, and it worried him slightly.

It took a surprisingly long time to find her. Normally Silver knew everything in his wood the moment he wanted to, but today its tangled pathways resisted him. "Is everything quite all right?" he asked politely when he finally located the dryad sitting on the banks of the Haller Brook. Water splashed over her long brown feet. She was curled over on herself like a small wooden statue, when at this season he would have expected her to be caught up in the Wood's jubilant fruiting, not yet quietening for the winter.

She showed him her pointed teeth. It was not a smile. "Bramble?" Silver said. "What's the matter?"

"Wickedness," said Bramble.

"Where?" Silver said. He had felt no stirring in his domain. "Tell me—I'll put Tobias to it. He'll be glad of the work."

The dryad shook her head slowly. It was a human gesture. She had a surprising number of those. "You are just like the other one," she said, "really."

Silver was truly offended once he realised what she meant. "In what way," he said, "could I possibly be compared to a criminal, a failure, a *monster* like Rafela? I am a scholar and a gentleman, and *you* are just a—a woodland creature, frankly. I don't know what makes you think you are entitled to pass judgment on me. Whatever it is, you are very much mistaken. What has even brought this on? Who have you been talking to?"

"Not talking," the dryad said. Her eyes gleamed with that odd light they got sometimes. "Thinking."

"It's not your business to *think*," Silver said.

Bramble hissed at him, and then she stood up with an abrupt splash, wrapped herself in the half-light and damp smell of the September morning, and was gone.

"Well," said Silver, "that was uncalled for."

He trudged back towards the Hall feeling disturbed and not a little upset, and found Tobias waiting for him.

He had a letter from Silver's mother. He'd asked the housekeeper to read it to him. He said this quietly and calmly; and just as quietly and calmly, he added, "She took on an old troll alone. Smashed her hip."

"I— Oh," said Silver. "Is—she all right?"

"Well enough," Tobias said.

"My dear—"

"Don't you *my dear* me," said Tobias, just as quiet, just as calm. He was a big man; he was a gentle man. He didn't *get* angry. Silver had never seen him angry. "She wrote to me for help, and I never knew about it. Don't you lie. I'll head to town on the next stage."

"I— Of course," Silver said. "Of course. You must be very worried. I'm very worried. She's my mother, you know. I'll come with you, of course, I'll—"

"You'll do as you please and be damned to you," Tobias said, in that same calm tone, and he shook his head hard, and he rubbed his hand over his eyes and let out a great shuddering sigh, and added, "There's no help for it. Never was anything but a fool, but shame on me all the same."

"Tobias, I'm—"

Tobias looked down at Silver's hand on his arm, and shook it off with one sharp movement. "You're as bad as Fay," he said. And then immediately, "No, I shouldn't say that, there's none as bad as Fay. But bad's bad enough; and I'm old enough to know better."

"It was one little lie!" Silver burst out. "Yes, very well, I confess—I omitted to mention—because I enjoy your company, because I wanted you with me—"

"You ever *seen* a bridge troll?"

Silver said nothing.

"Didn't think so," Tobias said. He scrubbed his hand over his eyes again, turning away. "Well, you're a pretty fellow, and a clever one," he said, "and I'm a fool as I said; but your mother was good to me when I would as soon have died, and I find I'd rather have her good opinion than yours, Mr Silver."

He took almost nothing with him. Silver had lavished him with gifts of good clothes and little luxuries ordered from town; Tobias left them all as if he had never even noticed them to begin with.

After he was gone Silver went back to the ground-floor room where he had slept more often, lately, than he had slept in the master bedroom. The bed was neatly made. There was an ewer of water on the bedside table. Silver took the unripe crab apple out of his pocket and threw it onto the bare floorboards. He *had* been making some effort to be circumspect about some things, within the house, but to hell with it. Henry Silver was only a mask after all; time to drop it. He was the Wood. He didn't need a housekeeper, or a cook, or whatever it was the rest of them did, Silver hardly knew. Let them all go back to Hallerton or High Lockham and forget he'd ever been here. He scowled at the little apple sitting sad and lopsided in front of the fireplace and made an abrupt one-handed twisting gesture.

It grew.

It grew, and it grew, and it grew, and it knocked the ewer off the table, and it turned the bed over on its side. When it could barely fit in the room anymore it put out flowers and fruit both together. Silver could feel the tree protesting against this uncomfortable business and didn't care. He went off to get rid of his staff, and so get on with the business of becoming a half-mad monster trapped in the woods for the rest of eternity.

NOW

While Maud was sleeping, Silver occupied himself with sulking. Fairyland lent itself well to sulking. Its flat dullness matched Silver's mood perfectly.

Even so, eventually he grew bored. He went back to the others and picked up a notebook to make another sketch of the arrangement of monoliths, but he must have taken the wrong one. He had not realised Tobias had also been making pictures of the landscape.

They looked very different to Silver's rough sketches—rather better, for a start. Tobias had managed to capture some of the sense of looming unpleasantness that the black stones carried with them. Silver found himself in the third picture, included for size beside the monolith he had been examining. He looked at it a little while: just a few strokes of a pencil, to create a dishevelled little figure with downturned mouth and sullen air. So that was how he looked. Well, it was how he felt, too. No one could accuse Tobias of being dishonest, now or ever.

"My apologies, Mr Finch," Silver said airily, turning back to their sad little encampment, "I seem to have taken your notebook rather than my own; if you could just pass me— *Damn*."

Tobias's whole large frame jerked an uncomfortable fraction when he spoke; he had been motionless before. Silver should have noticed that stillness. Tobias always found something to be doing. But even the jerk of his shoulders was slow, and when he lifted his head his expression was strange and dazed. The dark earth was covering his boots as far as his ankles, and one of his hands where it rested near the lifeless soil.

"Tobias—Mr Finch—*Tobias*," Silver said, panicking. Somehow he was at Tobias's side, he was taking hold of him. The hand that he pulled frantically away from the ground was chilled through. Silver clung to it, pressing it between his palms as if he might force warmth through his fingers. The soil around Tobias's boots was trying to harden into black stone like the monoliths. Silver said, "Stop—stop that," as if he were scolding a child, which was absurd. The dazed look in Tobias's eyes terrified him. "Get *up*," he said, because Tobias was too big and too heavy to be moved if he didn't choose to be.

"*Stop*," he said again, only this time he said it in that other language, the language that belonged to the Wood's memory, the language of old gods and dead wizards. "*I command you.*"

The creeping stone stopped its advance up Tobias's calves.

Tobias shuddered all over and then started to cough into his free hand, the one that Silver wasn't clinging to.

Silver had to let go of him. He backed off a pace, and then another. Tobias panted for breath, big shoulders moving. Then he stood, kicking away the black rock formations round his boots, and they splintered like glass shards. Silver opened and closed his hands a few times. He would have liked to take hold of Tobias just then; to feel for himself the warmth coming back into his chilled fingers. He had a terrible feeling that if he had spent only a little longer sulking, he would have returned to find just another black standing stone on the plain.

"Are you quite well?" he said. "What was that?"

Tobias worked his jaw back and forth a time or two

and said, "Bloody bastard *fairies*." He snatched up Maud's pack and checked the knives and the pistol at his belt. "Bloody, bloody, bastard fairies. Thanks." The last was abrupt. "Let's go."

"Go where?"

"It took the girl," Tobias said.

Silver hadn't even noticed. The patch of ground where Maud had slept curled into herself was conspicuously bare.

"Couldn't even shout," Tobias said, and he turned to Silver for a moment and said "Thanks" again. Silver looked at his grim expression, the tightly controlled line of his mouth and his white-knuckled fists, and thought of how many times, over the centuries, Tobias had watched and done nothing as an innocent was swallowed by the supernatural. He had to be busy, was how Silver had always seen it, but now the perception inverted itself and he thought instead: *He does not like to be helpless.*

"My dear—" Silver winced to hear himself. "Mr Finch—"

"Let's go."

~

The fairy had left footprints in the black earth, next to the solid marks of Maud's sensible shoes. The imprints of its long bare feet looked human enough to Silver: five toes, pad and heel. "If it was a man, I'd say he was starveling thin," Tobias said as they went. "Not enough weight there."

They were keeping to Tobias's pace across the empty country now. Silver had to half-jog to match his long strides. Tobias did not let up. He was still talking. "It wanted the girl all along. Probably *was* lurking some-where when we got here; that was an ambush. It waited for you to be looking the other way, didn't like the risk. They used to run from me when I was the wood."

"Did you get a good look at it?" Silver managed, out of breath.

"No. Came from behind me. Bastard bloody *fairies*. Silver and flint should do for it, but God alone knows what it's done with the girl."

Silver was shocked to feel a quite genuine stab of anx-iety for Maud—not the conjured ghost of proper feeling he'd managed to put together for the Maud Lindhurst he'd imagined back in Rothport, but a real twist of worry. He had never had a sister. Maybe he would be a less self-ish man now if he had.

The fairy's trail led a winding path through the mono-liths. For the first time since they'd begun exploring this place Silver felt as if they were actually moving, moving indeed faster and further than should have been possible.

His sense of the drowned wood, on the other side, as it were, of reality's curtain, was shifting too swiftly for ordinary space. He avoided looking directly at the standing stones. If he thought of Tobias kicking shards of black rock away from his boots like glass, he felt sick.

Then they came to the crest of a low hill and saw beyond it a small forest of monoliths, and in their midst a palace.

Here was civilisation, as Silver understood it. Here was the grand and the graceful, in the form of a gigantic dwelling-place all black arches and columns organised around a central plaza. But the palace was a ruin of collapsed walls and crumbled paving. A fine layer of black dust covered everything in view. Two sets of footprints cut through that dust, perfectly visible even from this distance: one person sensibly shod, and one with long bare feet.

In the middle of the plaza, covered in black dust like all the rest, was a dead tree, withered and grey. At the far end, open under the pink sky, was a dais. Six high steps led up to a throne that was nothing but a lump of black stone with intricate carvings about the base. At the foot of the steps, at the end of the trail of their footprints, stood Maud and her fairy.

Tobias took off at a run. Silver didn't even try to keep up with him. He was out of breath anyway. He picked his way across the plaza with care, circling broadly around the dead tree, which struck him as sinister. By the time he arrived at the dais, Tobias had the struggling fairy in a ruthless grip as Maud cried out in dismay.

It stilled when Silver came close. Silver could see now what Maud had meant when she said her fairy was *hard to look at*. It had that same half-present quality that the satyr had possessed, before Silver had killed it. The light slid away from its spindly form and only seemed to catch its eyes, which were glittering and grey.

"Good afternoon," Silver said to it.

The fairy hissed a word in what Silver supposed must be its own language. It was the same language he knew without knowing. The word was a remarkably rude one. Now he was close by the ugly throne, he could see that the marks on its base matched those he had found on a monolith halfway across the desert that was Fairyland.

They matched, too, the broken stones of a dead god's altar far away in Greenhollow.

Which meant that the being which Tobias had called the *Lord of Summer,* the monster Fabian Rafela had become, had begun as a fairy lord: which was just what Silver had first suspected long ago, before he was the Wood's creature, before he ever made a fool of himself over Tobias Finch, before everything.

And he had this in common with Maud Lindhurst: he did like to be right.

"What happened?" he asked, in the language of the living world, not the dead one.

The fairy writhed against Tobias's grip, but the big man held it firm.

"*Something* happened," Silver said. "Isn't that right? Because this *was* a kingdom, a mighty one, even, a kingdom of splendour and magic, and now nothing is here but the stones and the dust." He could see it, almost, the black palace all lit up under the still pink sky, the twisted tree in the courtyard crowned in green, the throngs of suppliants before the merciless throne in this place that had kept itself secret and strong and strange, on the far side of the Hallow Wood, long ago. "And there were many of you, and now there is only one. The others—"

"*Drowned,*" said the last of the fairies. "*All drowned.*"

"In the ocean?"

"*In time.*"

Silver nodded. He knew what the fairy meant. He had pictured it often enough, started to dream it—dreams that were maybe his own and maybe the memory of something else that had once occupied his own position. He had wept in fear; he had laughed and pretended it was not happening; he had written his monograph and published it; he had ignored letters from his mother; he had grabbed at Tobias and clung to him the way a drowning man might strike out for an outcropping of salt-drenched rock.

"*I beg of you,*" the fairy said. "*I beg of you, my lady,*" and Silver remembered that its first interest had never been *him.*

Maud was halfway up the dais, three tall steps above the three of them. Why hadn't Tobias noticed? Wasn't it Tobias's business to be alert to what, exactly, had become of the young lady they were supposed to be rescuing? But Tobias looked as shocked as Silver; he had not been paying attention. He had been watching Silver's face.

Maud took the rest of the steps in three long strides and bent to pick up the object lying on top of the throne. A crown, Silver thought, before he saw it. He wanted it to be a crown.

Maud held it up and it was a mask. It was made of some pale material so delicate that the dull pink light of Fairyland penetrated it through and through, giving it a faint rose colour. It showed an androgynous face with faintly bloated features and blank, staring eyes. A death mask, Silver thought. Someone had taken a cast from the bloating features of a corpse and created this mirror image to rest on the empty black throne.

Maud held it up with two hands, and then she looked down at the three of them, Tobias and Silver and the captured fairy, and her big watery eyes seemed distant and strange.

"Yes, of course," she said. Then she put the mask on.

It had no string, no hook, no fastening, but when she took her hands away, it stayed where it was. It was changing to fit over her long face, stretching out and rippling, the bloated look falling away as it clung and set over Maud's living features. She opened her mouth and the mask's lips parted. Then the figure on the dais let out a sigh, like someone terribly exhausted settling into a comfortable position from which they did not mean to rise.

Silver felt it in the land as the old power woke. The earth under their feet trembled and shook. A wind started to blow from nowhere, stirring up little storms of that black dust. The woman on the dais swayed on her feet. She blinked, once, twice, and the mask had had blank staring eyes with no holes to look through, but now Maud Lindhurst's watery blue eyes were set in that strange face.

She threw her head back and yelled. Silver could not tell if it was a scream of agony or a roar of triumph.

The fairy broke loose from Tobias's suddenly uncareful grip and fell to its knees. Its oddly glittering eyes had taken on a new gleam of dampness. Tears. "*Mistress,*" it said.

The woman whom Silver could not think of, now, as Maud Lindhurst turned her cold gaze down on it.

ILL-STARRED SLAVE, she said. *WHERE IS MY KINGDOM?*

Tobias muttered a heartfelt oath. Silver rather agreed with him. The Hallow Wood bred occasional dismaying monstrosities; his mother hunted terrors; he himself had once been the prisoner and victim of a fell entity which Tobias for one had counted as one of the old gods. The Lord of Summer had been a being of the same type as this dread lady, Silver could tell, but only in the way that a feral cat was akin to a tigress.

The Fairy Queen turned her gaze on the two of them. It passed over Tobias with scarcely a pause: *MORTAL,* she sniffed. Then her eyes met Silver's.

JACK OF THE WOOD, she said. *LITTLE BOY GREEN. WHOSE FLESH ARE YOU WEARING?*

"My own, madam," Silver said. "Which is more than can be said for yourself."

The Queen ignored this sally. *WHERE IS MY KING-DOM?* she said again. *WHERE ARE MY SUBJECTS? WHERE ARE THE THIEVES AND THE DANCERS AND THE LORDS OF EVER-AND-ALWAYS?*

"Drowned, I believe," Silver managed. The force of her attention was like a hailstorm. He wanted to put his hands over his face to shield himself.

DROWNED? DROWNED? I WILL NOT HAVE IT SO.

"Whether you will have it or not," Silver said, "it *is* so."

THEN I WILL REMAKE THEM, the Fairy Queen said. She lifted one of Maud's long-fingered hands and pointed it at the withered tree at the heart of the palace.

It erupted in green. Silver felt like a tug on his heart the gateway that opened past it and into the Hallow Wood. He thought of the fairy stories he had loved as a boy; how often they began with a traveller lost in the wood! But the fairies had never come from the Wood; they had come *through* it, through the Green Man's domain, from this dreadful place on the other side.

And the Queen would come through, walking among Silver's trees. She would descend like a black storm on a world of railway stations and steam tugs. She would have blood, again, as she had demanded long ago. The practical folklorists of Mrs Silver's acquaintance, quietly tidying up the confused remnants of the supernatural in a confidently modern world, would be as helpless before her as rats before a snake.

Silver found no secret well of courage within to defy her. He was a scholar, not a hunter. He thought she was fascinating; he thought she was astounding. He would have loved to somehow entice her into a conversation, even better if he had a notebook. He wanted to know who she thought she was, and where she thought she had come from; if the fairies really were a separate and magical species, or if as their looks suggested they should more properly be understood as human beings who had come under the influence of strong powers they did not understand. He wanted to make a grammar and a dictionary of her terrible earth-shaking language.

She was fascinating, and splendid, and *eternal*. Never mind clinging to a lover, or adopting an angry young lady, or keeping a cat; Silver could occupy himself forever in the service of the Fairy Queen. It would be service, obviously. She was not of a type to admit equals.

"Madam," he said, "if you are to pass through the Hallow Wood on your way, might I have the honour of escorting you?"

The Queen descended the steps at a leisurely pace and, with an air of enormous condescension, accepted Silver's proffered arm. It was still Maud's arm in his; she was still wearing her men's shirt. The face of the Queen had the bones of Maud's long face underneath it. Silver made himself smile at her. She was extraordinary, but she was a parasite of the worst kind.

"Shall we?" he said, and prayed and prayed that Tobias would have the sense to stay close.

They walked arm in arm to the tree, and through the twist in space and time, and into the Hallow Wood. The ground under the Fairy Queen's feet shrank away from her steps; the trees swayed away from her. "Just this way,"

Silver said. "Just so." He felt half as if he were coaxing a child, half as if he were trying to leash a rabid wolf. He kept his eyes fixed straight ahead. Out of the corner of his eye he could see Tobias and the fairy following them, one to either side, each eyeing the other mistrustfully.

"Ah," Silver said. "Here we are."

They stood among the still trees of the Hallow Wood at the foot of a steep escarpment thrown up against the horizon ahead like a wall. Everything was silent and dim.

THIS IS NOT THE WORLD, said the Fairy Queen. *I WANT THE WORLD. I WANT SERVANTS TO COME CRAWLING TO MY FEET. I WANT MY LORDS AND LADIES ABOUT ME. I WANT MUSICIANS.*

"In just a moment," Silver said soothingly. "Everyone will be very pleased, I am sure. Do you know, it has been hundreds of years, thousands perhaps, since anyone saw you, and yet people still tell stories of the Fairy Queen."

STORIES! the Queen repeated, and laughed.

"They can never quite capture," Silver agreed, "the effect of the real thing."

She turned to look at him, Maud's eyes in that cold, old face.

"I am something of a student of stories myself," Silver said. "Fairy tales—folklore—you know." Why would she know? Why would she care? "There is a myth, for example, of a great Inundation, common to many traditions, which describes the coming of a terrible flood." He licked his lips. "And then there is another which says if you are accosted by fairies in the wood, be sure to cross running water; they cannot bear it."

The Queen laughed.

"Quite, quite so; often these folk traditions are jumbled nonsense," Silver agreed. "But there is something worthwhile in knowing them all the same; something worthwhile in—oh, in study, and discovery, and so forth; in earning the respect of one's peers—for which one must of course *have* peers—and remember," he took a deep breath, "your name first, Maud, when we publish!"

And with that he reached out a blind hand in Tobias's direction. He felt relief shudder through him all the way to his toes when Tobias caught hold of it at once. Then he clamped his other hand firmly around Maud's arm, and let the drowned wood do what it had longed to do from the first and expel the living and breathing and *human* from its silent, eternal summer.

And the waters rose.

It had not been this way, Silver knew; not from a human perspective, anyway. The ocean had laid its long black fingers on the land slowly, rising a little one season and falling a little the next; the shoreline had marched inexorably inwards for generations, only now and then advancing in one great tide, far more often changing only a little, and a little more. But to the trees of the Hallow Wood time ran differently; and for them the waters had come as one single onslaught, without mercy, swallowing the forest and all the life it contained. So it came now, the dark gulp of the sea, roaring through the Wood.

The Queen screeched in fury and tried to pull away from Silver's grip on her. He was not a strong man. He was not a Tobias Finch. But her struggles were limp and unconvincing, the wildcat madness in her cries not matched by the strength of her movements, as if her body would not answer her commands. Then she tried magic, the dreadful power she pulled out of the very land; but Silver frowned, and the black water poured itself through and around the trees, swamped them, overwhelmed them, and they were gone. Where there was no Wood, her power fizzled out in darkness. There was no magic in this cold ocean, nothing for the ancient goddess to make use of. The Lord of Summer, Silver thought, in a wild reflection for which this was hardly the time and place, had been a parasite too. If he ever got around to rewriting his father's tables of classifications, he would have to take that into account.

The Fairy Queen twisted in his grip and spat in his face. Silver winced against it. He could feel her spit on his cheek; vile. He remembered with unfortunate hilarity that his handkerchief was filthy because he and Tobias had stood on the Rothport pier eating fried fish out of their hands. Tobias's hand was still holding on to him on the other side. He didn't dare look around, but there was no mistaking the strength and warmth of that grip. Silver was terribly afraid for him; for his careful, practical, thoroughly mortal life, his sound principles and good sense, his enormous shoulders and his hazel-green eyes and his hatred of helplessness and his excellent aim with a pistol.

TIME WILL NEVER HAVE ME, the Queen hissed. *NOR YOU, GREEN MAN. YOU WILL MEET ME AGAIN AND AGAIN. YOU HAVE MADE A DANGEROUS ENEMY.*

"I believe Time will have both of us, fairly shortly," said Silver, "unless you consent to depart this place. I do not imagine the sea will follow you home." Not a drop of water in Fairyland. "Miss Lindhurst will not be joining you."

SHE CHOSE TO SERVE!

"She did not have," said Silver, "the faintest idea what she was getting into. Eternal life among the old powers of the world is a fate I would not wish on my worst enemy, much less a bright young lady who had the misfortune to be curious." He strongly suspected that Maud had been the victim of some ancient enchantment on top of that; fairy-mad, as Tobias had said. Silver himself would have hesitated before putting on that mask. Probably. "*Now,* madam," he said.

The waters were gathered around them, a rushing blackness higher than their heads; not a tree remained in sight but the twisted one which the Queen had made her gateway between worlds. The Queen hissed at Silver again, but she was quite trapped. Her long fingers, Maud's long fingers, twitched wildly.

Then she departed. The living flesh of her face disintegrated into dust, and the dust blew past Silver's face in a sudden rush of foul-smelling air. He managed not to breathe in, and the wind of the Fairy Queen's passing blew through the darkness and passed beyond the Wood, beyond the world, back into her ruined kingdom. Her one surviving servant, the last of the fairies, scampered back after her. The twisted green tree abruptly dropped all its leaves when they were gone, and faded from view like a dream.

Maud let out a small whimper. It *was* Maud; her long, thin, not very pretty face, her watery eyes. "She was— She would have—" she said.

Then she fainted.

Silver entirely failed to catch her, but Tobias was there, suddenly, a big arm under Maud's limp weight. "Don't let go of me!" Silver said. The waters were still looming all about, on the point of crashing down over the three of them, and he did not know what would become of either of their fragile lives without him.

"I've got you," Tobias said, which was not at all what Silver had meant. "Can you get us out?"

"No," said Silver. "It's the ocean. It takes what it takes."

"Hm," said Tobias.

"So just—hold on," Silver said, and hoped and hoped that he'd guessed right. He took a firmer grip on Tobias's hand and put his other arm around Maud. They stood there in a strange huddled embrace, three small fragments of life at the base of this ancient stony escarpment in the midst of a world being swallowed by water. He could feel the very last fragment of the Wood holding out against all hope; little islands, he thought. There had been little islands, crowned with stiff trees: but the right birds had not come, or the great elk had not been by, or the soil had turned salt-choked and worthless, or—there were a thousand ways for a wilderness to die.

Silver closed his eyes and said, to this last fragment of the drowned wood, *That's enough.*

Everything ends.

With a terrible crash, the black waters closed over them all.

～

Time was unforgiving stuff. Silver looked up, somehow, in the midst of its roar, and saw the black stone rising on the hill above their heads. For one awful moment he was sure it was the palace of the Fairy Queen and she had found a way through after all.

Then the building resolved itself into the stern arches of Rothling Abbey, and for a few moments—a few centuries—that lonely dwelling-place stood firm on the headland, and every storm off the sea broke with a crash on its high towers.

Only a few moments. Silver watched it crumble, feeling a terrible ache of sadness in his throat. He thought of the old vampire, the old Abbot, creeping out at dusk to watch the child Maud playing among the ruins; lurking in the shadows of the town, and throwing the bodies of young men in the water. Rothport was coming into being now, first as a scatter of fishermen's cottages and then as a market and finally, smug and confident, extending its modern pier out into the waters, acquiring its attendant tugboats, its row of gas lamps, its smart terrace of wealthier houses rising up along the hill towards the church. A piece of the future, Rothport.

Silver let out a shaky, relieved breath. "There," he said.

He and Tobias were standing among the sharp rocks at the base of the cliff, with Maud a limp weight between them. Rothport's dreary little beach stretched away from the base of the rocks; they would have to paddle through the shallows to reach the town, but that was a minor inconvenience. It was, so far as Silver could judge, an hour or two after dawn.

He was not actually supporting any of Maud's weight; and now they were here and safe with the Fairy Queen far away in her own kingdom, there was no need for Silver to be hanging on to the others this way. With immense reluctance he let go of Tobias's hand. He would have liked to hang on a moment longer, trying to memorise the warmth and strength of it and the feel of the big man's calluses. But it was done, it was done. Everything ends.

"We had better take Miss Lindhurst home," Silver said. "My mother will be pleased."

As he stepped away from Tobias and straightened up his tweed jacket, he turned his face out to the water. But not so much as a whisper of the drowned forest remained. Silver could not feel the faintest trace of it. Oh, he was a poor steward for the Hallow Wood, that was sure. What *would* Bramble think?

"I'm sorry," he murmured to the great silence. "I had to."

Tobias was looking at him askance. Silver gave him a bright, empty smile and said, "Shall we?"

~

They took Maud home. Silver this time was actually

paying attention to the parents, so he could tell that she got her long face from her red-eyed mother, her watery eyes from her pompous father. These were the parents Maud had spoken of so scornfully. They didn't understand; they would take her books and send her for rest cures. But they had paid Mrs Silver's by-no-means-limited fees, and they looked terribly relieved to see their daughter alive.

Silver set himself to be charming.

In ten minutes he had them eating out of his hand. He was such a clever young man; a very bright fellow indeed; he had taken such good care over our dear little girl—

"The fact is, Mr Lindhurst, Mrs Lindhurst," said Silver, "after her dreadful ordeal, I think Maud needs some expert attention. I hesitate to suggest—because, you see, it would really be doing *me* a favour—but my dear old mother, as I am sure you have noticed, is not in the best of health." He bestowed a limpid smile on Maud's mother, who leaned a little closer towards him. He could *feel* Mrs Silver's eyebrows going up behind him, but he did not look round. "I have often thought that some *feminine* companionship would be just the thing for her," he said.

~

"*What* do you think you are doing, Henry?" said Mrs Silver, when the Lindhurst parents had departed all wreathed in smiles and left them to confer among themselves. "Feminine company! If you mean to *punish* me for having the effrontery to involve you when you were busy having one of your sulks—"

"Maud Lindhurst is very bright, knows far too much, and is sure to get herself into trouble again if she is left here alone," Silver said. "And she beheaded a nine-hundred-year-old vampire with a kitchen cleaver just this week, so I'm sure you'll have lots to say to one another. Please, Mother." He gave her a smile. "For me."

Mrs Silver sniffed. "The charm didn't work when it was your father doing it, young man, so don't think you can bully me."

"It's true enough," said Tobias abruptly. "The girl'll get herself in trouble again if nothing's done."

"Even you, Mr Finch?" said Mrs Silver irritably, and then, "Oh, very well, very well! I suppose if you *both* insist."

"Wonderful," Silver said. "Oh, and I meant to ask. Would you be willing to give me a haircut?"

~

Freshly shorn, almost presentable, Silver returned himself to Greenhollow Hall. He did not bother with the travelling part. He went into the Lindhurst family garden, and he walked between two trees, and he was home.

Greenhollow Hall, from the outside, looked as if no one had lived there in centuries. It had never been exactly a *beautiful* house. Perhaps the mediaeval hall had been attractive in a foursquare way, but it had been added to patchwork-fashion over the centuries, developing wings and cupolas and even a small pointless tower like an unfortunate youth developing boils. As far as Silver could tell, no one with any sense of grace or proportion had ever been consulted on a single one of the additions. Honestly, the creeping vines swallowing the place improved it, if only because they suggested some sort of unity of purpose.

It was just as well that Silver had no intention of trying to set up the place with a staff ever again, because he could not imagine anyone consenting to work in such a ruin. What a look he would get, if the redoubtable housekeeper he had originally employed saw what had become of it, and how quickly!

The main entrance opened into the now roofless great hall. Silver went in through the side door that led into the wing where he and Tobias had kept their bedroom. The apple tree he had commanded into being in the height of his sulk was still in fruit and flower there, unhappily. "I am so terribly sorry," Silver said, and laid a hand on its trunk.

With a nearly visible shudder of relief, the power of the Green Man passed away from it. A flurry of white blossoms fell at once, and most of the fruit too, with a rotting stench. It would be kinder to take the roof off this room too, so the tree could get some more light and build up its strength. Silver settled for a good tug through the ivy that had taken up residence on the eastern wall, which fell apart into dusty fragments of brickwork at once.

He picked up the ewer that was still on the splintered remnants of the floor. A large spider scuttered out of it and fled among the tree's twisted roots. Silver laughed softly. "I apologise," he said to the tree, "but may I—"

It gave him one more crab apple, small and sour. It probably wouldn't fruit again for years. Fair enough, really. "Thank you," Silver said.

Then, since he knew the way of it now, he opened a door through the Wood and walked the hidden pathway into Fairyland.

The palace of the Fairy Queen was unchanged; only the black dust had resettled itself over their footprints, as if it had been months or years and not two days. Silver climbed to the throne and looked thoughtfully down at the mask that had re-formed itself there. What an extraordinary artefact. He would still quite like to sketch it, but he did not think he would come back here again willingly. Maybe in nine hundred years or so.

"I can see you," he said, in the language of the dead, as he descended the steps.

The fairy—Maud's fairy—was standing in the shadow where one crooked column had half-tumbled against another. Silver could mostly see the grey glitter of its eyes. He thought of the satyr that he had somehow summoned out of God-knows-where—maybe some other beyond-and-further place like this one—and how it had solidified as it died with an apple in its heart like a silver bullet. "You weren't always like this, were you?" he said. "There used to be more to you."

The fairy came forward slowly.

"Here," Silver said, and tossed it the crab apple. "Unfairy fruit. If you want it."

The fairy looked at the throne.

"She does not seem like the best of mistresses," Silver said. "Though I am no expert."

"*I have nowhere else to go,*" the fairy said.

"The Wood welcomes you, as it welcomes all the lost," Silver said. "It may not treat you kindly; it is the Wood. It may not keep you safe; it is the Wood. It will not last forever, but it will last long enough; and the trees grow, and the seasons change, and the wild things come and go, as do the monsters." He nodded at the crab apple. "Try it. Sour, probably, I'm afraid; it's out of season."

"*I will consider,*" the fairy said. It was a sensible being, Silver thought: thinking, speaking, from a civilisation unknown to Man, at least for most of the last ten thousand years; a civilisation that had perished somehow and left nothing but a throne and a mask and a dry country. Perhaps Silver would find out how, someday. Perhaps he should press the fairy a little harder. But he felt sympathy for it, sympathy and not a little fellow-feeling. He gave it a polite half-bow of farewell and went home.

∾

And the months of spring and summer went by. Silver walked the Wood. His only concession to humanity was to visit his library occasionally. He would really rather not lose his books to rust-mould and white mushrooms; not yet, at any rate.

Bramble seemed to think better of him than she had in a while, though with a dryad it was always a little hard to know. Silver attempted actual conversation with her a few times, but they only succeeded in confusing one another.

Then came the August day when the dryad came to him adorned with early blackberries and said, "He is here. He came."

Silver's first thought was of the fairy. Bramble shook her head—that human gesture! How like Tobias she was. Silver would be able to look at her, and remember, five hundred years from now.

Then he said, "Wait, Mr Finch is here?"

"Yes!" said Bramble, with an exasperated air, and a stray tangle of her thorns caught in the flesh of Silver's hand and tore a red gash there. *"Come."*

"Of course—don't fuss—I'm coming," Silver said, wishing mostly to avoid further thorny expressions of the dryad's urgency.

It still took him a rambling while to find his way back to Greenhollow Hall. When had he last been there? The days ran together like a dream, and he did not often sleep. Had it been a month?

Had it been more?

The sun was setting when Silver walked out of the wood. He found Tobias standing before the ruin of the Hall with a sober look on his face.

"Mr Finch!" he called out.

Tobias turned and his expression flickered: he looked relieved and stricken all at once. Silver was caught at the heart by it. Had it only been a few months ago he had inwardly railed against Tobias's imperturbability, his enormous calm? It was somehow more upsetting now to see him robbed of it, if only for an instant.

"Whatever is the matter?" Silver said. A whole collection of human concerns rushed back upon him at once and he felt a chill. "—is it my mother?"

"What? No, she's well," Tobias said. "Well enough. Hip pains her sometimes. She's thinking of retiring."

"How unlikely of her," Silver said, but he smiled, reassured.

Tobias smiled back for a moment, the same small smile that Silver had once treasured as his own particular possession. Not for very long, all things considered. Their intimacy had lasted only a span of months. He was still glad to see that smile, though it vanished after an instant and was replaced by another flicker of expression: embarrassment, maybe. And then stony calm again. Dear Tobias, always the same. "Doubt she will," he said. "Not with Miss Maud dragging her hither and yon."

"So Maud is well too," Silver said. "How glad I am to hear it. Then what brings you to Greenhollow, Mr Finch?"

Tobias closed his eyes a moment. Silver took him in. He was not unchanged by the time that had passed; his hair had grown a little longer, and he'd grown a beard to go along with the moustache. It suited him. There was a trace of grey at his temples, too, which had not been there before; that suited him as well. He'd always been a handsome man.

"Mr Finch?" Silver said.

Tobias spoke abruptly, as though the words were better out fast and over with. "Came to say we may as well trade."

Silver said, "What?"

"It never bothered me," Tobias said. "The time, you know. The loneliness. Never gave me all that much trouble. I kept a cat." His jaw worked. "There was Fay, mind, and that wasn't so pleasant; but he's good and gone. Just the wood left, and I know the wood. Plenty to do. Left it a little late in the year to settle for the winter, but I wanted to see Mrs Silver comfortable, and Miss Maud. She's a good girl. Takes to the work nicely. And it's not as if you need to be a big fellow for the hunting; not if you know your business and you keep your silver and flint to hand. So that's that."

Silver stared at him.

This was the way of it, he thought, with Tobias Finch: he said nothing and said nothing, kept quiet and watchful for month after month, but all the time under that stolid exterior he considered things deeply and carefully, and deeply and carefully and with uttermost patience he decided what he would do, and then if he possibly could, he did it: because he could not bear to be helpless. That little speech had been almost nothing but practicalities, one thing after another. Tobias had offered to return himself to the service of the Hallow Wood as if it were only something to be sorted out, the way he used to sort out his firewood, his vegetable garden, his trapping and his mending.

But Silver *knew* Tobias, he did; their liaison had been brief but their friendship had not, and he knew that the last time he had heard Tobias come out with a speech that long, he had left Greenhollow the same afternoon; and the time before that, Tobias had kissed him.

He had been wrong, to think Tobias could not imagine it, and could not understand: enormously, absurdly wrong. After all this Tobias had seen, and understood, just what it was that Silver feared so dreadfully. How simple his solution must seem to him. For four hundred years he had lived alone as the Wild Man of Greenhollow and managed well enough. Four hundred years with a cat and a demon for company! And now he proposed to resume that quiet existence without a murmur, and count as an advantage the mere absence of the demon.

"Mr Silver?" Tobias said.

Silver said, "Absolutely not."

Tobias furrowed his brow. "I—"

"I know I was selfish," Silver said. "I am—I admit it—a selfish man. And I know that I lied to you. I don't even believe I'm sorry, though I doubt I would do it again. But—my dear—I am not quite so selfish as that. And the truth is that I do fairly well these days, if I say so myself. I believe the difficulty was trying to live both ways at once, as it were. To be a man within Time and beyond it all at once was . . . uncomfortable. But to take you out of the world again, just for my own relief; to rob you of human voices and human faces and all the things of this time and this place—Tobias, that would make me as cruel a friend as your Fabian once was." He summoned a smile. "And I like to think I am not quite as bad as all that."

Tobias said nothing, and said nothing, and licked his lips and said nothing, and then he took two steps forward and took Silver in his arms and kissed him.

Silver was not expecting it. He was speaking into it at first, and then he fell into startled silence, lips parted. The kiss only went on for a moment. Tobias's lips were chapped and warm, his beard and moustache faintly coarse. Silver had not kissed anyone in more than two years. The sensations fell back into place as if their last kiss had been just yesterday.

When their lips parted, Tobias's arms were locked close around him, his hands clenched in the sleeves of Silver's shapeless tweed jacket. "You wore my coat," Tobias said, as if it were terribly important. "You're still wearing my coat."

Silver had honestly stopped thinking of it as Tobias's coat at some point in the course of the long summer. "My dear," he said, quietly, and he put up a hand and wiped away the dampness on Tobias's cheek. "I would be only too pleased if you would like to stay a little while. But I won't have you stay forever. It won't do, you know."

"It's not right," Tobias said.

"It is what it is."

"You should have—your books, and your papers, and things," Tobias said. "Firelight and music. Friends. You're a young man—you've got plenty to be doing—"

Silver couldn't bear it, so he kissed him. Tobias clutched at him as if he might disappear. The August evening was still and warm around them; the whole Wood was still and warm, as if this instant of touch and care might last forever, stretch itself out into an eternal and changeless summer.

"You," Tobias said, when they parted, and he touched the side of Silver's face, his ear, his hair. Silver understood that *you* to mean *my dear,* or *sweetheart,* or—all the things Tobias could never quite say. He caught hold of Tobias's careful hand and kissed his knuckles. "Wouldn't you be better off going back to town?" he said. "I am sure my mother can manage without you, but it would set my mind at rest, I think, if there were two sets of eyes keeping a watch on Maud."

"She wrote you a letter," Tobias said, in a tone as close to wheedling as Silver had ever heard from him. "She's been at your father's diaries, and there's naught Mrs Silver can do to stop her. Been writing to some Continental fellow as well. It's ghosts she's onto now."

Silver laughed, and shook his head, and said gently, "I'll read it later."

Tobias said, "Please."

Bramble was watching them from the shadow of a young hawthorn close by. One could hardly expect a dryad to understand the concept of *private conversation*. Silver stepped out of Tobias's embrace regretfully and said, "I think you should go."

He would weep about this himself, later, he thought; when he read Maud's letter, perhaps, sitting in the library he was determined to preserve for as long as he could, he would weep for another self he might have been—someone for whom the world was young and full of possibility, someone who would write and study and take himself on ill-planned adventures and discover all things marvellous. But he was not the least bit tempted, all the same, by the bargain Tobias proposed. He had glimpsed eternity in the drowned forest, and it had opened something up inside him which could not bear to be any smaller than he already was. And by God, it would be a terrible smallness, a terrible selfishness, to force upon another man a fate he could not bear himself.

And Silver thought of the dry ruin of Fairyland and thought: *There are worse eternities than the Wood.*

"*Yes,*" said another voice, answering the thought, "*there are many, many worse.*"

"Hoi!" said Tobias, sharply, and grabbed hold of Silver's shoulder, trying to draw him back. Tobias would put himself between *anyone* and danger, given the smallest opportunity. His other hand already had a pistol in it.

"It's all right," Silver said.

The fairy was recognisable mostly by its eyes, which still had the same grey glitter as the first time Silver had seen it. Its body had changed. Before it had only been possible to get a sense of a lean figure standing there *somewhere,* like a shimmer of reflection in a sunlit pool. Now it was a solid figure, as tall as Silver was, starvation-thin under a patched robe that hung loose from its narrow shoulders.

Silver could not help noticing that its ears were *not* pointed. A loss for the illustrators of his childhood fairy tales.

"You ate the apple," he said.

The fairy nodded. It took a careful step forward. A

ring of white mushrooms sprang up around its feet. Silver frowned at them. *"Give me the greenwood,"* the fairy said.

"I beg your pardon?" said Silver.

"An owing. A repayment. Go with your lover, and give me the greenwood. It will be wild, and it will be strange, and it will endure. It is the Wood."

Tobias swore in a low voice. He was still holding that pistol.

"That's . . . very kind," Silver said. "But the Wood is not mine to give. It doesn't belong to me at all; in fact, I believe it's almost the other way around. And if you thought to make yourself another Lord of Summer, I could not permit it in any case."

"No lord I; not in a thousand thousand years. I have served before. I am a faithful servant. Charge me with it. Give it to me. Shall I endure in your debt always?"

It was genuinely upset, Silver saw. "I am sorry," he began.

"You were unhappy," said Bramble.

Silver startled. He had almost forgotten the dryad was there. He felt Tobias start as well, the little jerk of his whole body, and that startled him too. Tobias had always known Bramble better than he did. But there was proof, if you needed it, that Tobias did not owe the eternal forest another moment of himself; that he belonged to the human world, and quite right too.

"I thought you had planted yourself," said Bramble. Out of the shadow of the trees she came, heavy with blackberries, knotted and strong and taller than any of them, which was new. "I thought you would grow well here. We are not wicked. We are not"—she said the unfamiliar word with difficulty—"*monsters*. But then you were unhappy, and you sowed more unhappiness, and it was wickedness upon wickedness."

"What on earth are you talking about?"

"Now, then," said Tobias.

"Hush," the dryad told him firmly. She turned to the fairy. "I am the wood," she told it.

"The queen?"

"No," said Bramble scornfully, "the *wood*."

"Ah. She never did quite say what she'd decided on," Tobias murmured. "Not like a dryad, you know, not to have its own particular tree."

"I can serve you well," said the fairy.

"What for?" said Bramble. "Live. Grow. Change. Last. It is enough."

She turned her gaze back on Silver, and hesitated a moment; then she caught his hand a moment in her strange clasp. Silver yelped as thorns bit into his skin again and tore threads from the tweed jacket. Bramble lifted his hand up and forcefully shoved it down again. Silver made a strangled sound—trying not to laugh—when he realised this was her version of a firm farewell handshake.

And his chest felt hollow with uncertainty, amazement, and not a little sorrow: and as simply as that, the Wood let him go. He felt the change. His feet seemed suddenly to stand a little heavier on the earth, and his sense of the summer evening shrank around him. Rather than a great inchoate knowledge of warm air and warm earth and longing for rain, he was only a man; and, he noticed, he had been bitten by one of the evening's host of winged insects, square on his ankle where the hem of his trousers was going ragged.

"Will you come back?" Bramble asked.

"Probably . . . not," Silver said. "At least, I think, not in the way you mean." He ached suddenly at the thought. To be free of the Hallow Wood meant to be free of its secrets and strangeness. He would take no more walks through Time and beyond it. If he ever sketched the Fairy Queen's mask, it would have to be from memory.

The dryad nodded. Then she went to Tobias, and touched his shoulders with both her thorny hands. "Foolishness!" she said, and let out her odd gurgling-water laugh, which Silver had heard very seldom.

"Now, miss—"

"Not *miss*," said Bramble, and she smiled, baring all her pointed brown teeth.

And then she and the fairy were gone; disappeared in the space of a breath, leaving only the circle of white mushrooms where the fairy had stood. Silver knew the way that was done; how between one instant and the next you might drop yourself into the slow time of the wood and be gone. He knew, but the knowledge was faint and sideways. He could not have explained it, or written it down. He could not have done it himself.

"Well," he said, and then his eyes fell on the vine-choked ruin of Greenhollow Hall, and he burst out laughing.

"What's the matter?" said Tobias.

Silver turned towards him and said, "My dear—my dearest—" and kissed him.

It had only been meant as a quick expression of affection, but Tobias took the kiss and made it tender. It went on longer than Silver had meant. He did not mind in the least. Tobias had offered to return to the wood for his sake.

"It's only," Silver said, when they broke apart, "where *am* I going to live? In my mother's house, I suppose! I'll have to pack all my books. *You* can carry them. Oh, it's going to be crowded." The house in town where Silver had passed his boyhood was respectable but not splendid. "And she and I *will* argue, you know. We can't help ourselves."

Tobias coughed. "Miss Maud's in the second bed-room," he said.

"Oh, is she?" said Silver lightly. He bestowed his most winning smile on the big man. So Maud Lindhurst was looking into the question of ghosts! *He'd* wanted for *years* to know more about ghosts—he'd never seen a ghost—he hadn't had much opportunity lately—after all, whoever heard of anything haunting a tree?

"She is," Tobias said. "And I'm in the third."

"Well, then. Since it seems there's no other option," Silver said, to Tobias's little smile and the growing brightness of joy in his eyes, "I hope you don't mind if we share."

Acknowledgments

With heartfelt thanks to:

My agent, Kurestin Armada, the best advocate an author could hope for.

My editor, Ruoxi Chen, sine qua non.

The Tor.com Publishing team: production editor Lauren Hougen, copy editor Richard Shealy, proofreader Shveta Thakrar; David Curtis, who somehow outdid himself with even better cover art this time, and Christine Foltzer, the art director; Irene Gallo, publisher and creative director; and Mordicai Knode, Caroline Perny, Amanda Melfi, and Lauren Anesta, for the amazing work they put in on marketing, publicity, and social media.

Emma, A. K. Larkwood, and Everina Maxwell, whose support and encouragement saved this book from certain doom.

Jenn Lyons, who gave me kind words when I really needed them.

The Armada, the Sack, and the Ballydaheeners; love to you all.

Mum, Dad, Paddy, and Oli, for everything.

Luke, always.

About the Author

Photograph by Nicola Sanders

EMILY TESH grew up in London and studied classics at Trinity College, Cambridge, followed by a master's degree in humanities at the University of Chicago. She now lives in Hertfordshire, where she passes her time teaching Latin and Ancient Greek to schoolchildren who have done nothing to deserve it. She has a husband and a cat. Neither of them knows any Latin yet, but it is not for lack of trying.

TOR·COM

Science fiction. Fantasy. The universe. And related subjects.

*

More than just a publisher's website, *Tor.com* is a venue for **original fiction, comics,** and **discussion** of the entire field of SF and fantasy, in all media and from all sources. Visit our site today—and join the conversation yourself.